FIRES OF PROMETHEUS

MICHAEL G. THOMAS

First published in the United Kingdom in July 2011 by Swordworks Books.

ISBN 978-1906512774

Typeset by Swordworks Books
Printed and bound in the UK & US
A catalogue record of this book is available from the British Library

Cover design by Swordworks Books
www.swordworks.co.uk

FIRES OF PROMETHEUS

MICHAEL G. THOMAS

CHAPTER ONE

The first Biomechs were encountered during the campaign to retake the Titan Naval Station. It wasn't until the ground offensive on Prime however, before their true potential was realised. What started as small-scale usage of suicidal fighters quickly turned into the tactical use of the larger models in assault operations. The Biomech itself became an army of options and opportunities.

Evolution of the Biomechs

Kerberos was quiet, much quieter than any of the military personnel could have expected. Almost three months had passed since the end of hostilities in the Proxima Centauri System between the Confederate military and the insurgents under the guidance of the Church of Echidna and her militant allies. Though open warfare had stopped there were still sporadic skirmishes and suicide bombings as the insurgents did their best to spread fear and terror in the civilian population. None of the underlying issues had been resolved and the entire sector had settled into a period of uneasy truce, a kind of space based phoney war where both sides were preparing and waiting for the resurgence of battle.

Of the eleven planets in the System the four that were colonised had seceded from the Confederacy. Many of the others teetered on the brink of joining either through fear of what might happen if they didn't or simply because they lacked faith in the Confederacy to keep them safe. Fort Hood and Confederate military outposts on the other colonies were on full alert and had been since the attacks on the Titan Station that precipitated the start of open hostilities. Of the colonies that split from the Confederacy, none recognised the authority of the Army, Navy or Marine Corps and most had given demands for military forces to leave. Their occupation of colony land was considered an act of war that could lead to the continuation of the war. Admiral Jarvis, the Supreme Commander of all Confederate forces in Proxima Centauri, had given the order than no state land or bases were to be relinquished and that support would be provided to any forces needing assistance.

To the men and women at Fort Hood, deep in the heart of the enemy camp, these seemed to be empty words. With just a small number of combat troops the fort couldn't be expected to hold out for long if a concerted attack was launched against them. Common sense dictated they evacuate the base and move their units into orbit, but the Navy was refusing to move them. As they waited they could only hope the threat of full-scale colonial warfare between the Confederate colonies and the secessionists would stop both sides pushing for what could become a genocidal conflict. Colonel Towers, an imposing figure and commander of the base, stood in front of a paper map of the area and traced out a number of geographical features not far from their walls.

"If you look here there are four locations where units can be concealed close enough to strike at the walls. We can reach two of them with indirect fire but these two are a real problem. I want remote gun systems positioned here, and here," he explained as he pointed to the locations on the map.

"What about the cover on the access road to the south?" asked one of the lieutenants.

"That's already covered. We have a foot patrol out there right now setting up a checkpoint and OP. With these areas covered we should get at least fifteen minutes warning of any ground approaches to the base."

"Captain, will this give us enough room to get your air units down safely for resupply?" he asked looking across to the small group of Navy personnel stood in the corner.

Captain Erdeniz stepped forward and examined the air corridor provided by the defensive weapons and counter measures. It was his job to ensure the meagre air support they had available was able to bring supplies and aid in when needed. But as the noose around them tightened it was becoming more and more difficult.

"It isn't perfect but it is big enough to get the small craft down in one piece. If we need to evacuate in a hurry we'll have to bring in the big birds, for that we'll need suppression aircraft to keep missiles off our backs, Sir."

The Colonel turned to look at the assembled officers.

"The situation here is going to hell, I think you all know that." The rest of the officers were surprised by his candour and at least one chuckled at his comments. The Colonel tried to spot the laughing man but the room quickly quietened down, much to his dismay.

"You've seen the reports, the same as I have. The insurgents are thick as thieves with the so-called Church and a good number of the unions here. With offers of free medical support, work for those that want it and free housing it's not surprising the masses are going for it. Hell, if I hadn't seen how they are doing this I might even be interested myself. Be under no illusions, gentlemen, the enemy can only achieve their objectives by turning the colonial population into docile servants who will do what they are told and when. One day they will understand this and then it will be much too late."

"Sir, I don't see what politics has to do with Confed military forces? Can't we just leave them to it?" asked a junior officer.

"Leave them to what exactly? Evict us from our bases and disband all colony militia forces so that their biological monstrosities can take over. A population that is unable and unwilling to defend itself will cease to be free. Mark my words, any colony falling for the promises of these people will turn into a slave worker's paradise in just months. It gets worse though, they do not seek to simply remove us," he said shaking his hands in anger, "these bastards want to replace us! They hate us with pure, unreasoning hatred and they will not stop until our very way of life is destroyed. You saw the video of the fighting on Prime. They will take by force that which they cannot take by the ballot paper."

He signalled to one of the Naval Intelligence officers standing at the front.

"Sir, if you look at the big picture it is clear the merging of the political parties, and the sidelining of religions outside of the Church, is creating a dictatorial one party system on Kerberos. This model is spreading through the colonies of Prime and outwards to the other worlds. The bottom line is that it's easy to just say yes. The enemy is offering an end to hunger, unemployment, illness and even the requirement to defend yourself. The offer is to turn humanity into soft, docile cattle. We have studied our enemy in detail and it gives me no pleasure to inform you that this insidious danger is the greatest threat the Confederacy has ever faced. Even worse, our citizens are welcoming it with open arms!"

The Colonel acknowledged of the officer's comments and then returned to his position. His body language suggested he was trying to inspire but it looked more like he was preaching. It wasn't helped by the fact that of all the officers in the room, he was the only one that had yet to face the enemy in battle.

"As you know we have been given the order to stand. This is a Confed base and we are not handing it over to insurgents, religious fundamentalists or some Kerberon nutjob who thinks he is the second coming of Christ. This base has already been given a final ultimatum by representatives of this Church of Echidna who say they are operating as intermediaries on behalf of the Kerberos government. That's bullshit, as you already know there is no government here anymore! They are just puppets for this religious cult that will not stop until every colony does the same. I've received word from the Fleet and they confirm that since the deadline passed every base in the System has been waiting. So far nothing has happened. Return to your units and re-check their readiness. Something is coming, I can smell it and when it does we need to be ready to act."

A chorus of salutes and agreements echoed inside the

small room and was followed by the removal of the men as they rushed to check on their troops. The first planet to secede had been Kerberos and it was generally considered to be the second planet in the System. Since the rise of the Church it had taken on greater importance to the level that it was now seen as the hub, the centrepiece of the new secessionist movement.

As the officers streaked out a grubby looking soldier rushed in carrying a map. His uniform was that of one of the scouting units with tiger stripes camouflage pattern and light equipment optimised for speed and discretion.

"What is it, Corporal?" asked the Colonel.

"Our patrol in Sector Five has come under attacks from colonial units from Yama City. Our unit made it back but we lost a squad out there, Sir."

"What the hell! Why did you leave them?" he shouted as he stormed to the doorway leading to the open compound. The young soldier chased after him.

"We were ambushed by almost hundred people. Rocket fire destroyed our first APC, we were lucky any of us made it out alive!"

Colonel Towers stopped and looked down at him. His face was contorted in anger and worsened as he spotted the patches on the soldier's arm indicating his last two tours of combat.

"Let me tell you, son. Just because you've been out in the dust getting your ass shot off by some local bushwhackers, it doesn't give you the right to abandon your men out there."

"But, Sir!"

"Don't 'but, Sir' me, soldier! I know my duty and we never, ever leave our men behind. Now come with me, we have work to do!" he shouted as he continued onwards. As he stomped off a solider leaned over from the top of one of the watchtowers.

"Colonel, there's a vehicle heading towards us!"

The watchtower was located in the corner of the barracks and was the tallest structure in the entire base. It was raised about five metres higher than the perimeter wall, but like the rest of the compound was only recently built and lacked the thicker walls and strong defences normally seen on military bases. The entire compound was initially only supposed to handle up to a thousand personnel. Now it was overpopulated, containers and vehicles were packed into the smallest of spaces as the units posted to smaller camps had flocked to this larger site. A sergeant, recognisable by his beret and shoulder stripes, marched out into the open parade ground near the walls and started barking orders. He was quick and efficient, in less than two minutes the walls were manned and the troops were ready. From one of the concrete bunkers rushed a four-man squad to the reinforced gateway and took up positions around it. They were not like the frontline combat units that had been fighting the insurgency the last months. They lacked the close fitting armour of the Marine Corps or even the heavier, more old-fashioned carapace suits still used by regular army units. These men and woman wore their standard combat fatigues with basic protective armour vests and plating over the key body parts. Two hundred years ago this kind of gear would have been considered common, now it was barely adequate for riot control. The Colonel stood fuming as the combat units waited for the inevitable fight. He had work he wanted to do and dealing with another non-issue was the last thing he needed. Two of his guards moved out of the command centre and took up positions behind him. Sergeant Wilkinson stopped in front and saluted.

"Sergeant, what is it?"

"Sir, a small group in an armoured vehicle. They're flying a white flag and approaching our gate."

"Why are you wasting my time with this nonsense, Sergeant? Captain Erdeniz is in charge now. Find him! I have more important things to do than chasing locals waving flags!"

"Where the hell is Captain Erdeniz?" he demanded, only for the young man to appear before him from the weapon stores. It was obvious he had been collecting gear as on his shoulder he carried a standard issue L48 carbine. He was a naval officer who, along with hundreds of navy crew, had been sent to the surface for leave while the warships were repaired and patched up. Though the fighting had ceased for some time the troubles were far over. Following the epic space battle at Prime there were hundreds of dead and wounded personnel. Far more than could be managed in the space docks and stations operated by the Navy. The sporadic bases and barracks on the colonies were still officially Confederate territory and like foreign embassies they were considered sovereign soil.

"I've just received word that a unit has been hit out on the lower checkpoint. Watch the walls and don't let anybody in, I will deal with the checkpoint incident and bring back our boys. I am leaving you in charge, don't let me down." He tapped the officer on the shoulder and then marched off.

Captain Erdeniz was stunned and forgot to even reply. As a naval officer he was used to commanding groups of gunners, or assisting in engineering and technical operations. Commanding the potential defence of a major fortified base on hostile territory was something he had never trained for. This Colonel must have something of a death wish. Rumour on the base was that he had missed out on the fighting and had something to prove. From the shouting display he heard it seemed the man had a real chip on his shoulder.

"Asshole, it's people like you that get people like me killed!" he muttered as he chased after the officer.

"Colonel!" Erdeniz shouted, but the Colonel was already too far away to hear him as he approached the landing pad where three Cobra Transports sat with their engines running.

From the outside the Cobra MK II looked like an angry bug. The wings lifted up high with four powerful engines fitted on rotating mounts to provide vertical take off and landing capability. It had no obvious weapon systems fitted and could easily have been a civilian craft if it wasn't for the camouflage pattern and military markings. The craft was only capable of atmospheric flight and had a range of just a few hundred kilometres. It was small, barely big enough to carry eight men, but its speed and agility made it perfect for rapid insertion and extraction of troops. The front of the craft was bulbous and appeared to contain more glass than metal. The looks were deceptive though and this craft more than any other was the favourite vehicle used by Army Special Forces for the last twenty-three years. The engines were already powered up when the Colonel arrived and the sound was high pitched, almost screeching. The Colonel jumped inside to be given an intercom headset so that he could speak and hear over the noise of the engines.

"Sir, we're heading to the checkpoint now. Last contact was three minutes ago. According to the radio operator multiple vehicles hit them and rocket fire has destroyed their transport. The unit retreated to a depot building where they are trying to hold back the attackers. The last message was on an open channel and said they were being overrun and needed immediate assistance," explained the co-pilot.

"Come on then, they haven't got time and neither have we!" barked the Colonel as he strapped himself in, the pilot turned to speak to him.

"Uh, Sir, it isn't necessary for you to come with us."

"Did I ask your opinion, Lieutenant? I will not let any of my boys be taken by those snake obsessed bastards, now move it!"

"Sir!" The pilot hit full power. "What about support, Sir? Transmitting on an open frequency is against regulations and could indicate their position has already been overrun."

"Bullshit. Are you trying to scrub the mission? Either you get me there or get out!"

The co-pilot looked over to the pilot who gave him a whimsical look before turning back to continue on the flight.

As the craft blasted away Captain Erdeniz was left covering his face from the dust. He looked about, trying to assess the situation and quickly walked over to the Sergeant who seemed to know what he was doing. Fort Hood was certainly no vacation spot but it did provide a relatively quiet place for over six hundred injured men and woman to rest and nurse their wounds. The fort was positioned on the outskirts of Yama City on the planet Kerberos and over twenty kilometres from any other settlements, yet the young Captain felt thousands of kilometres from the calamity that had been taking place in recent months.

"Good work, Sergeant, I'll take a look,"

"Be my guest, Sir."

Captain Erdeniz moved up the rough steel ladder near the main entrance much more quickly than the local enlisted men would ever have expected, taking a high position so that he could examine their immediate surroundings. As he stood at the high point he felt like a commander on an ancient Earth battlefield waiting for an unruly horde to come rampaging towards them. In his hands he held a pair of image-stabilised binoculars. They were low tech but in this area the highly magnified image was just what he needed. Through their lenses he watched the approaching vehicle at close magnification. The vehicle was six-wheeled and looked like one of the transports used by the Marine Guards unit on the planet.

"Sergeant, get ready, this could be trouble! I want the perimeter sealed and get air support on standby. This is probably just another scouting party but it could be something much bigger!"

Erdeniz looked very different to the rest of the infantry on the base. He was slight and until recently had been a mere lieutenant on board the flagship of the Confederate Battlefleet in the Proxima sector. His posting aboard the Battlecruiser Crusader had given him ample opportunities to indulge his interest in unconventional weapon systems.

Prior to their action at Titan he had successfully tested a form of canister rounds for the ship's railguns. He was far from ordinary, though due to his exemplary service and bravery he had been promoted to captain and put in charge of the primary gun decks on the warship. In theory this was a major achievement, but he was still convinced it more likely substantial losses suffered retaking the Titan Naval Station made it inevitable that many officers would be promoted to replace those killed or wounded. His two weeks leave on Kerberos however had been anything but relaxing.

"Captain, shall we get a drone up?" shouted the Sergeant.

Captain Erdeniz paused for a moment. The base was already low on ordnance. Zealots had destroyed a large number of the unmanned robotic drones in a raid three weeks earlier, leaving just four. It was just too risky not to use them though so he gave the order before turning back to his view through the binoculars. The vehicle was about five kilometres away now and kicking up a dust trail behind it. As he examined it more clearly he spotted a number of other small vehicles following behind it.

"Put me through to the Colonel!"

Before he could be answered a great flash from the centre of the base indicated one of the rocket-assisted drones was being launched to around a thousand metres. As it hit its preselected height the jet engine kicked in and the robot raced off into a circular path over the base. In less than ten seconds a series of pulses on the Captain's electronic datapad signalled an active video feed. The device on his belt was standard equipment for officers in the military and was a ruggedised version of the common computer and communications kit used on many colonies. It combined an encrypted communication system along with live video feeds, encryption tools and command control for many of the base's automated systems such as fire suppression and surface to air weapons.

He pulled up his pad and entered his hex based security code to gain temporary access to the system. It was a nuisance but after several risky operations it was deemed critical that no digital systems stayed connected and authorised for more than twenty minutes to avoid their use by the enemy. The display flickered as several windows appeared with maps, videos feeds and tactical overlays for the entire area. On the right hand side an icon flashed from command, he tapped it to reveal a full size video link to the Colonel.

"Captain, I've only just left. What's the problem?"

"Sir, we have multiple targets converging on the approaching vehicle, I recommend you return to the base before they are able to bring portable surface to air weapons within our deployment zone."

"I don't see the problem. If they are hostile then open fire. If they are friendly, look after them. Don't call me again, Captain, unless you have actual news to report, out!"

"Asshole," muttered Erdeniz under his breath reviewing the video feed from the drone.

"Sergeant, you getting this?"

The Sergeant had his datapad resting on the wall as he surveyed the distant dust patterns. He looked down before turning back to the Captain.

"Yes, Sir, it looks to me like the lead vehicle is being chased."

"How can you tell?"

"Well, I've been chased before and if you look at the speed they are moving they aren't worried about taking chances."

As if to emphasis the point a series of cracks from rifle fire echoed through the open and quiet valley.

"Stations, keep your heads down, boys!" shouted the Sergeant as he lowered himself, keeping a careful eye on the vehicle.

Captain Erdeniz double-checked the drone feed and with a deft tap brought the video camera in for a closer look on the nearest vehicle. The truck filled the screen showing about a dozen people, as well as masses of boxes and crates lashed to the bed at the rear. There were no obvious weapons though no doubt the boxes could conceal all manner of evil. He double tapped and then pulled the zoom back into a wide-angle mode. He quickly spotted over twenty vehicles, some were just small three-wheel affairs, others were much larger and all carrying armed citizens.

"This isn't good."

From his position along the wall he could see half of the base. To his left the wall went back several hundred metres until it rose up slightly on a small hill. Behind him was the main command centre and barracks building and to the side of that the motor pool where around twenty armoured vehicles waited. Although some were fully operational, most were being worked on by the engineers. To the side of the command centre was the landing pad for light aircraft. The walls were now manned by an entire company of soldiers, mostly Army but with a smattering of Navy and Marine units mixed in with them. A second company was split between working on the vehicles and patrolling the rest of the perimeter. A small contingent from the Army manned the mortars and base defences. Turning back to the approaching trouble he tapped the intercom unit on his ear.

"Platoon commanders check in," he ordered, waiting for confirmation of the tactical deployment of his perimeter forces.

"2nd Platoon in position, light machine guns ready to go, Sir."

"3rd Platoon, we have two squads on the walls, third will be ready in less than a minute."

He waited for a moment, waiting patiently for 1st

Platoon, nothing happened though.

"1st Platoon, where are you?" he demanded.

There was still no reply and for just a second he worried they may have gone rogue. This had happened on two other bases, where combat units had defected to the local forces. This was usually down to money or pay but some just didn't have the stomach for what could be a bloody last stand. As he tapped the intercom to call again an apologetic voice was on the comms channel.

"Sir, 1st Platoon is now on the wall, we had a slight, ah, ammunition problem."

"Really? Well, check your feeds and watch your angles. We'll deal with this later."

"Captain, they're in range!" shouted one of the men from the tower.

On the datapad the perimeter of the base showed up as a green vector image with triangles indicating friendly units and small circles showing automated or sentry controlled weapon systems.

"Standard rules of engagement, fire if fired upon. Watch for friendlies and keep an eye on your buddies," he said, trying to be as calm as possible.

"Launch the floaters!" called one of the lieutenants.

The unflattering nickname was for the special artillery shells that were launched up several thousand metres and then loitered in a shallow glide for up to fifteen minutes. A simple tap on a command datapad would send the shell back to the ground with an accuracy of a few centimetres vaporising the target with a precision high explosive warhead. It was a simple system giving the forward commanders the closest thing to their own air cover but with immediate availability. A series of low thuds signalled their launch though they were impossible to see or even track as they hurtled skywards. The clatter of bullet impacts spread along the outer wall as a burst of fire from the approaching vehicles struck the reinforced concrete and metal structure.

"Shall we respond, Sir?"

Captain Erdeniz wasn't convinced though.

"Hold fire. I repeat, hold your fire! That might not have been aimed at us. Wait until the truck is inside our fire zone. If anything else passes the three hundred metre barrier you are clear to respond," he said as he moved along the wall.

"Sir, they'll be at the gate in thirty seconds!" shouted the Sergeant.

Captain Erdeniz lifted himself up higher as he watched the truck move to the gate. For a few seconds he thought it might crash directly into the armoured door and he braced himself for impact. Luckily the driver jammed the brakes on at the last minute and the vehicle swung around and stopped in a cloud of dust and debris. From the back a number of scruffy looking civilians as well as three men in police uniforms jumped out. One looked up to Captain

Erdeniz and signalled with his hand to get his attention.

"Lieutenant Inspector James Cooper, requesting sanctuary!" Without waiting he started to help the people from the back of the truck.

Captain Erdeniz shouted down to the men in the courtyard to open the gate. His attention was drawn back to the approaching horde as the large number of vehicles rushed headlong towards their position. The nearest were two and three-wheel vehicles. All were civilian and carrying far more people on them than their design intended. Behind them were now more than twenty trucks and large wheeled vehicles. Some appeared to be police issue, the rest a mix of civilian and commercial, all with people on them and many of them armed.

"Get ready!" shouted the Sergeant.

A chorus of safeties being clicked off and bolts pulled back indicated the conversion of the defenders from a static force to one ready to repel any and all attackers. Captain Erdeniz looked back to his datapad and the video image from the small drone circling overhead. The back of one of the trucks was carrying a fixed weapon mount, it was primitive, possibly a relic from the Great War but still capable of shredding through the concrete and steel wall of their compound. Then he spotted it. The truck following it carried a similar fixed weapon mount, but it was a twin surface to air missile system of the type fitted around the Presidential Palace to protect against missile and aircraft attacks.

"Crap!" he muttered as he grabbed his intercom.

"All units..." he started before the clatter of bullets and cannon rounds peppered the wall forcing him to the ground to take cover. As he fell he dropped the datapad and almost landed on it. Luckily for both of them the device was sturdy and protected by a laminate layer of metal and rubber. As he grabbed the device two soldiers carrying rifles moved around him.

"I'm okay, not a problem!" He assumed they thought he must have fallen.

One of the machineguns on the tower opened fire and in less than three seconds the entire wall lit up with scores of carbines and rifles adding their fire to the approaching vehicles. An unguided rocket whistled overhead and crashed down into the centre of the base, hitting an already damaged truck. Captain Erdeniz looked at the drone video on his datapad to check the tactical situation. From the feed he could see the enemy dismounting and taking up positions several hundred metres from the compound walls.

"All units! Hold your fire! Watch for muzzle flashes and hit them with long range ordnance. Everybody else keep your heads down!"

One thing he knew from naval combat was that using all your fire at the first opportunity just wasted ammunition and gave away valuable information to the enemy. They had the better cover and the longer ranged guns. In this scenario it was in their interest to let the enemy do the work.

"Unit commanders, check your datapads for target identification and acquisition."

A chorus of acknowledgements came across the tactical network as their precarious position was quickly shared along the personnel defending the perimeter. More fire bounced along the wall though the sturdy material easily absorbed the small arms fire.

The main compound gate opened along with a series of tones to let the guards know the base was being opened. As soon as a gap a metre wide appeared a stream of women and children rushed inside. Captain Erdeniz shouted down from the wall, waving at the barracks infirmary.

"Corporal Weather, get them to the infirmary and check them out!"

The Corporal waved to three other men who helped escort the party away as yet more rushed inside.

"Sir, this man says he needs to speak with you!" shouted the Corporal pointing to the nearest ladder for the man to climb.

As the last of the fourteen civilians made it inside the marines quickly sealed the doorway and returned to their positions. More shots came in and the video feed displayed two groups of the enemy making their way closer to the walls by staying low in the rocky depressions.

"Lieutenant Jones. Permission to access the floaters?" asked the leader of 3rd Platoon.

"Do it," replied the Captain over the intercom before selecting the open channel.

"All weapon systems authorised, clear the perimeter!"

With that simple command the access to the base automated weapons mounts, artillery and drones was immediately turned over to the platoon commanders. It was quick and efficient and the results almost instant. Three explosions about three hundred metres out caught the first group moving into position. The aerial floating shells struck without warning and instantly halted that attack. As more shells were launched from the automated launch system a man in partial police clothing reached him on the wall.

"Captain, I'm Special Agent Johnson, attached to Naval Intelligence. I need to speak with the Fleet as soon as possible, I have urgent information for Admiral Jarvis."

"The Admiral?"

A rocket propelled grenade slammed into the wall and blew out a chunk of masonry that blasted two men from the wall. One landed hard and didn't appear to be moving.

"Medic!" shouted Erdeniz, though he didn't need to as a group of marines were already heading to the injured men. The man that had hit the ground hardest was crying out. Erdeniz turned back to the newly arrived agent who was also watching the casualties with a morbid curiosity.

"It's the quiet ones we need to worry about. You said you needed to speak to Admiral Jarvis?"

"Yeah, you know her?"

"I should do, I'm part of the Crusader's crew and we have met a few times."

"Really? Interesting. Anyway, thanks for taking us in, we hit a spot of trouble!" he said with a lopsided grin.

Several more rounds clipped the wall a few metres from where they stood but already the amount of fire was decreasing. As each of the floating artillery shells launched downwards less of the attackers were inclined to push forward.

"I can get you a signal to the Crusader in orbit. She'll have to bounce the signal to the office of the Admiral. What is it about?"

"I can't say, I'm sorry but it is too delicate. Let's just say that this information is critical to the Confederacy, that's why we were trying to get to you."

"What about the people with you? What's going on?"

"They are two of my colleagues who I can trust and their families. When they discovered we were still in contact with Naval Intelligence they stormed our police headquarters. Either we bugged out or we would have died with the rest."

"Who are 'they'?"

"You've not heard? Colony defence has been handed over to the Biomechs under the command of Echidna operatives. All paramilitary personnel have been forced to hand in their firearms and report to work placement centres for allocation of new duties."

The datapad on the Captain's side started to emit a tone indicating a new message from command. He lifted his hand to pause their conversation. As he examined the screen it cut to a video link to the Cobra MKII Colonel Towers had left off on. The Colonel was speaking into the device as he hid behind what looked like a piece of blackened metal.

"Captain, it was an ambush, they were already dead. My God, all of them!"

The video picture started to shake and it looked like the Colonel was moving but it was soon obvious that the ground near his position was shaking. Flashes followed by the familiar crump of heavy weapon fire erupted and the picture went dark grey. As the image went a series of howls and low noises, as if from a wild creature, came over the speakers.

"What the hell is going on down there?"

Johnson looked unfazed by the sounds and sights of what was happening on the display.

"It's Biomechs, once you hear them you never forget them, Captain."

For a brief moment the picture on the datapad changed, the Colonel had either moved it or it had been knocked aside. As the image stabilised it was clear what had happened. Several bodies in Confed uniforms lay scattered about the rubble. The bloodied face of the Colonel filled a third of the screen and in the background stood three Biomechs, three metre tall monstrosities, each bristling with tight fitting armour and weapons. The screen flashed and the feed went dead. Captain Erdeniz turned his head in anger before straightening his back and tapping his intercom.

"Platoon commanders, meet me in the command centre. Squad leaders, hold your positions and watch your zones. Nobody, and I mean nobody, comes anywhere near the base, out!"

He moved to the ladder and started to climb down. Special Agent Johnson approached and pointed down to the ground as though he was asking a question.

"Yeah, come with me, I think we have things to discuss."

CHAPTER TWO

The origins of Spartan are still a mystery. Few records exist other than the brief mentions of his upbringing and family. The first confirmed records concern his time as a pit fighter where he achieved fame and notoriety as one of the toughest and most versatile on Prometheus. Many doubt his meteoric rise to glory could ever have occurred without this strong lesson in combat and resilience.

The Rise of Spartan

Spartan couldn't see in the pitch black of the room, but he could smell the dampness and sweat that reminded him that his situation wasn't improving. He opened his mouth to speak but nothing came out, his throat was parched and nothing other than a few croaks staggered out of his mouth. His head was pounding a mixture of either a long drinking session or because he had been pounded in the head by somebody's fists. As he struggled to remember, a light was switched on that for half a minute completely blinded him. He lifted his hands to shield his eyes to find he was chained and shackled to the wall.

"What do you want?" He tried to shout but again it came out as a muffled groan.

"Sergeant Spartan, terrorist, murderer and soldier of the fascist Confederacy. Have you made your decision?" A blurred shape of a man stood in front of him. Spartan struggled to remember, just a mixture of lights and faces with pain and violence thrown in. He needed a more time to collect his thoughts. As he desperately tried to think the voice continued.

"For your own safety we have moved you from Kerberos. Where you go from here is up to you. We already know you work for the Confederate Marine Corps. Those days are over now, Spartan. The days of the Confederacy are numbered, soon the dawn of a new, civilised and equal age will spread through Proxima."

At the mention of Proxima some of Spartan's memories flooded back. The uprising and insurgency orchestrated by the Zealots, the militant wing of the Church of Echidna and the collaboration of the Marine Guards unit on Kerberos. Finally, he remembered finding the murdered President and his cabinet at Yama City. He swallowed several times, trying desperately to clear his throat.

"I...I remember..."

"You remember? Good, then you can tell us. What does Admiral Jarvis plan to do about the secession of the colonies on Kerberos, Prime, Orthrus and Agora?"

"I'll tell you what she told me..." He turned to look at the changing shape of the man facing him.

"Good, I thought you might change your mind. So, tell me, what does she plan to do?"

Spartan simply stared at him, saying nothing.

"Well, what does she have to say to us?" he asked again, this time more firmly.

"Fuck you!" Spartan shouted and then spat on the floor. The man took a step forward, presumably to strike Spartan but somebody stopped him before he could get close enough. Another two men appeared, one wearing some kind of wide headgear approached him as the rest spoke quietly to each other.

"The Confederacy has gone, Spartan. The only holdouts in this entire sector are Avagana and a handful of the smaller colonies through the Rim, Prometheus and the gas giants. With the habitable planets now free how long do you think it will be before the rest join us?"

"Join you? Who the fuck is you?" laughed Spartan. "You're a bunch of old religious nobodies that want to line your own pockets. You'll replace the Confederacy with your own ideology!"

The small group of men had stopped talking and all

moved around Spartan. The tallest spoke first.

"The Church of Echidna offers a new union for those who seek the redistribution of power and wealth to the people. Before this year is out every colony in Proxima will join our family, that shouldn't concern you though. For your crimes our leaders have decreed you and your friends should suffer."

The man with the hat continued.

"A man with your skills could be of great use to us. This is your last chance to avoid a terrible and just fate. Fight with us or die in the pit fights like the rest of the dogs! Your choice!"

"Just kill me and get on with it!" Spartan was already trying to work out how he could turn the situation to his advantage. Planning and strategy had never been his strongest points but he was strong and his reactions generally excellent. He was convinced he could at the very least cause a lot of damage if he could get his hands free. As he twisted his arms it was obvious the chains were much too tight for him to wriggle out of. He looked about the room, his eyes now almost fully adjusted to the light. It was a small room and more people were tied up just the same as he was. He recognised the shape of General Rivers in the corner though he wasn't moving. He was about to turn back to his chains when he spotted a glimpse of movement. It was small, so small that if he hadn't already been looking at the old General he never would have seen it. The man blinked with just the one eye. Spartan squinted, making sure he had seen correctly, then the General did it again. Spartan nodded gently and then moved his eyes away from him and back to the guards.

"What about them?" He looked towards the other prisoners.

"That is none of your business, murderer!" said one of the men.

Spartan glanced again at the prisoners, looking for signs of people he might know.

"Come on, did you set them up as well? You bastards!"

The man started to laugh, it was a low chortle but the self-satisfaction was evident. As he continued Spartan could feel his heart increasing in rhythm, his blood felt like it was going to boil with pent up rage and anger. He pulled hard at the chains and succeeded in doing nothing other than giving his tormentors more to laugh about.

"You should save your energy, you will need it where you are going. As for the rest of them, well, they've all told us what we need to know. They will be meeting with the slavers shortly. Either they work in the mines or fight in the pits. One way or the other they'll be dead in a few months..." he said and then looked deep into Spartan's eyes, "...as will you!"

Spartan thought back to his comrades back in the Fleet, so many of them had been killed or maimed in the fighting. Of all of them though he missed Teresa the most. He'd met her during his training on the Santa Maria that at the time had operated as both a training and transport ship for the Marine Corps. She had been injured in the battle to retake the Titan Station from the insurgents. With all the trouble since then he'd been unable to spend much time with her and after the debacle on Kerberos he was doubtful he'd ever see her again. It was that final thought that pushed him to try something, anything that could get him away from wherever he was.

"I'll join..."

The men stopped talking for a moment, each of them looking down at him. They waited for him to speak again. Spartan coughed, took in a deep breath and continued.

"If you're right, what do I have to lose?"

The tall man leaned in closely again, this time Spartan could see the spittle dripping from his mouth as he leered.

"If you join us you will have to turn on your precious Confederacy. Can you do that, soldier?"

"I don't care about the Confederacy, I want to see Teresa again."

"Teresa?" asked the man in the hat.

"Private Morato, it seems she was his lover on his ship..." He then turned away to say more but Spartan couldn't hear.

As the group spoke Spartan looked back into the room to look for anything he could do or grab that might help him. The walls were bare metal and the only objects were the dark plates on the one side of the wall that he assumed must be one-way mirrors. If so this was a cell of some kind, though according to them they had left Kerberos. It must be a prison transport vessel then, he thought to himself. He started shouting.

"Look, get me out of these and I'll do whatever you want, I can't take this any longer!"

He lifted his arms so that the chains went taut and rattled as they scraped along the floor. The man with the hat said a few more words until the tall man seemed to be in agreement with him. He then returned to Spartan and placed a key into the lock. Leaning forward he grabbed Spartan by the arm and lifted him up. He groaned a little from the pain in his left leg, an injury he didn't even realise he had. From the corner of his eye he spotted two men in the ceremonial armour of the guard unit that betrayed the President back on Kerberos. He tried his best to hide the contempt he felt towards the traitors.

"Now, Spartan, if you are to join us we must first..." said the tall man before he realised what was happening.

With a speed that surprised them all, Spartan delivered a savage uppercut to the man that connected under his chin and knocked him out cold. Moving before the guards could intervene he grabbed the second man and locked his arm, twisting him in front as a human shield.

"Let him go!" shouted one of the guards as they entered the room, both pointing their carbines at him.

Spartan looked at their gear, noting that they were using L48 carbines with the small calibre box magazines fitted. They had limited capability and were perfect for military use on ships where penetration was an issue. He felt a pang of anger towards them with their pretence of being an elite and loyal part of the Corps, when the only thing they had in common with his compatriots was the equipment. The man squirmed, trying to move away from Spartan but a simple squeeze on his left arm forced the man to keep still, Spartan's strength being much more than he could cope with. At the end of the room he could make out General Rivers, he looked unconscious but Spartan knew better. In the last few seconds the man had already turned slightly towards him and winked, letting him know he was ready.

As the guard moved a little closer he reached just a metre from the sitting figure of the General. Spartan gave him a gentle nod and like a coiled up snake he struck. His hands were still bound but his lower body was free. With all the power he could muster the officer smashed his foot into the back of the guard's knee. With a crack the marine tipped backwards and collapsed to the ground, firing a short burst as he fell. Spartan took the chance and pushed his prisoner forward as he dropped low and ran to the fallen man. The second guard tried to get off a shot but the stumbling man crashed into him, blocking his line of sight for just long enough to allow Spartan to reach him. Though his body ached from the hardship he had endured he found new strength. Sliding along the floor he crashed into the man quickly grabbing his head and twisted his neck, snapping it instantly. He picked up the man's carbine, flicked the safety off and as he turned aimed it at the guard.

"Drop it!"

The rest of the men that had been speaking to Spartan ran from the room leaving just the guard. As they rushed away he could hear their footsteps becoming fainter and fainter. Both had a clear shot available to them though Spartan was acutely aware that he was totally unarmoured whereas the guard wore a full personal defence suit, also known simply as a PDS. It was a complete self-contained body armour package that tightly moulded to the wearer's body. Armour was provided to all key parts of the body and was proof against small calibres and shrapnel. The suit was also tied into the digital battlespace system used by the Confederate military and this provided up to the minute tactical information, mapping and communications.

"We have more armed guards on the way. Drop the gun or I'll put you down!"

"Fuck you, if I drop the gun you'll shoot!"

The two stood in silence carefully looking at each other, waiting for the hint of a movement to indicate that one of them was about to shoot. On the ground the General was trying to wriggle free but his chains were not going to break, no matter how hard he tried. Spartan needed to do something fast before the rest of the guards turned up. He could go for speed but there was a good chance he would be shot even if he fired first. The carbines could spit out small calibre rounds in massive numbers, then how could he help General Rivers? If he were dead he'd never see Teresa again. With that final thought he made his decision and turned the muzzle away from the guard.

"Okay, okay...I'm putting it down, don't shoot!"

The guard was taking no chances and tensed slightly, expecting something bad to happen. He pulled slowly on the trigger, ready if the moment required it. Spartan knelt down lowering himself slowly to the ground. Pushing his hands out he placed the carbine on the floor and then stood up, pushing his hands out in front in a gesture of compliance. The man moved forward.

"Stay there!"

Spartan's hands were head height but as the man approached he lowered his hands very slowly until they were at his waist. As if in surrender, he maintained the stance with his hands pushed out and the palms facing the man. For a moment it looked like the guard was going to wait, but gaining the upper hand seemed to go to the man's head and slowly but surely he moved closer to Spartan.

"Hands! On your head...Now!"

The guard lifted his carbine up higher on his shoulder, aiming a little lower into the middle of Spartan's chest.

"Come on...... two more steps!" whispered Spartan to himself.

As soon as he was near enough Spartan pushed his body out to the left and snapped forward. His right hand grabbed the side of the carbine and pushed it away a few centimetres. Almost as soon as his hand hit the metal a blast of flame roared from the muzzle and multiple rounds flew out to the reinforced metal bulkhead. Stepping towards the startled guard, Spartan smashed his left hand up in a hammer grip underneath the carbine. It looked almost like a showpiece move as the carbine flipped up and around so that the muzzle now faced the guard. Spartan released his grip and took hold of the weapon, their roles now reversed he made no attempt to stall for time and simply pulled the trigger. The first few rounds took chunks out of the man's chest armour so he held down the trigger. As the rounds hammered home they tore a hole in the plating. The guard was blasted backwards by the weight of fire before slumping down to the ground.

The General called out from the far end of the room.

Spartan didn't wait and he moved directly to him.

"Are you hurt, Sir?"

"No, just get me out of these things, we need to move!" Fire had already returned to the eyes of the veteran commander.

Spartan pulled his chains taut and told him to get back.

Pointing the weapon at point blank range it only took

two rounds to shred the chains and to free the General. As soon as they fell away he moved forward and started to strip ammunition from the dead guard. Spartan took two more clips from the second fallen man and checked for anything else that might be of use. As he rummaged through the suit he was dismayed to find the man carried nothing other than his personal weapon and a side arm. Thrusting the pistol into his belt he turned back to the prisoners, many of whom were now watching them though none said anything. Spartan knelt down to the first, a haggard looking man with a bruised face.

"Why are you here?"

"I...uh...no idea. I was working in the steel mills when these creatures attacked us. I've never seen them before, they killed some of our people before men in armour arrived and took us prisoner. We've been here for weeks now...might be longer, I can't tell you anymore."

As Spartan listened to the man he tapped him on the shoulder.

"I don't know what's going on, are you able to fight?"

The man, weakened both physically and mentally, tried to move but lacked the willpower to push himself.

"Stay there, we'll do what we can." Spartan stood up and looked about the room.

"Spartan, we need to go!" General Rivers said impatiently.

Spartan was tempted to leave but a nagging doubt in

his mind told him to check. He moved along the rest of the prisoners, looking for anyone who might be able to help. As he passed the weak wretches he noticed a number of them watching him, some with anger in their eyes. Halfway a long he spotted a familiar face.

"Marcus?" The man said nothing so he knelt down and shook him, he was covered by a blanket. Spartan pulled it back it reveal he was covered bruises and cuts.

"Bastards!"

He stood up and called out.

"We're going to fight our way out of this place. If anybody wants to join us lift your hands. If you stay here all I can promise you is a slow death at the hands of these animals. Who will fight with us?"

A few hands went up, yet half of the prisoners failed to respond. Some were simply too weak, the rest were probably scared or had no idea what was going on. It didn't really matter. Right now he only needed people who were of use. Spartan moved along the line, destroying the chains with the carbine. When his job was done he looked back to see five haggard but motivated men stood waiting to hear the plan. General Rivers was near the half open door and looking down the dark corridor, waiting for the inevitable arrival of more guards.

"How many weapons have you got?"

The General turned back and waved his carbine at Spartan who then turned to the five men.

"Check the guards, see if you can find anything else."

The men moved like a pack of wolves and stripped any equipment they could find from the two bodies. It didn't take long though for them to show just one knife and a pistol. Spartan remembered he had an extra pistol in his belt, taken from the first guard. He reached down and pulled it out.

"Here, take this one."

A short man, probably in thirties but actually looking much older, reached out and took the weapon. As it was placed in his hands he pulled out the magazine, checked the rounds, replaced it and cocked the weapon.

"You've done this before?"

"Army Special Ops, back in the day," he replied before moving over to the General to watch the door.

Spartan was relieved that they had at least one other person with combat training. He looked down at the still unconscious figure of Marcus. His gut told him to get moving but the thought of leaving a comrade as loyal as Marcus pulled at him.

The General calling for them to leave snapped Spartan out of his thoughts.

He paused just for a second. It was simple, if they were victorious he would come back, if not, well, it wouldn't matter then would it?

He checked the magazine on his own carbine and drew back the bolt, pulling another round into the chamber. The bullets looked odd, as they were a self-contained caseless bullet and propellant. Perfect for use in all atmospheres and temperatures producing no wasted materials when used. Spartan moved forward and joined the small group assembling near the door.

"Have any of you seen the rest of the ship? Any information we can use?" the General asked.

The man Spartan had spoken to previously raised his hand.

"I've been down the corridor. They took me there for tests a few days ago. About thirty metres down on your right, the soldiers came from a room a bit further along. Other than that I don't know."

"Right, Spartan, I suggest we get ourselves some more weapons. We could try for the soldiers' room, probably a barracks of some kind. Either that or we try for blades in the room where they did the tests."

"I say we hit the barracks room and fast. A few knives won't help once they get here and they've been gone for several minutes. There could be more on the way already, Sir."

Rivers agreed and without waiting Spartan moved off, the carbine lifted to his shoulder and ready to shoot. The two men with pistols followed along with the other three men and General Rivers brought up the rear. The corridor was plain, though a number of unusual markings were placed every few metres on the walls and coloured lights ran along the floor. Spartan stopped, raising his hand. General Rivers and the ex-soldier dropped down to the floor. The other four quickly copied them, sensing danger but unsure as to what they should do. Further down the corridor great noises came, it sounded like men shouting and it was becoming louder. From around the corner at the end, near to where the expected soldiers' room was, four soldiers appeared. Rather than checking first they rushed into the corridor and started running towards the room with the prisoners, therefore directly towards Spartan's group.

"Now!" shouted Spartan.

Aiming low he pulled the trigger and immediately felt the continuous shake of the weapon on his shoulder. The smaller calibre recoil was modest and he was able to release a thirty round burst that struck the first three soldiers with unnerving accuracy. The ex-soldier aimed carefully and squeezed off three rounds, the first hit the weapon of the first approaching guard but the second two struck the same man in the chest. It was a short but violent burst of fire and in seconds the three guards were down and groaning in pain. Spartan moved forward, still keeping his carbine tucked into his shoulder and aimed ahead, ready for any potential threat. The fourth man had ducked back and inside the room but in his haste had not shut the door.

Without hesitating Spartan ran inside to find the soldier pulling a weapon from the rack on the wall. The room was small and contained bunks for six people, no more. Spartan rushed towards him, firing his carbine until it ran out of ammunition. The solider staggered back under the weight of the bullets but was still standing when Spartan reached him. Lifting his weapon he slammed the butt of the gun hard into the man's stomach, forcing him to double over. Lifting the weapon he brought it down like a club onto the back of his head. Looking around there were a number of thermal shotguns on the weapons rack as well as two lockers of ammunition and a large amount of clothing and armour. He moved forward only to be interrupted by pistol fire. He half expected more guards to enter the room but instead General Rivers and two of the prisoners came in.

"The corridor is clear for now. What have you got?"

Spartan looked at the General and grinned, "Guns, ammunition and even better..."

He picked a piece of hardened black material from the wall and pulled it over his chest.

"Riot armour!" answered General Rivers with a matching grin.

The armour looked like something you might use for sport. It featured a simple padded muscle chest plate with matching shoulder pads and upper arm protection. Spartan pulled two straps, instantly tightening the fit around his body.

"They've got eight sets in here, more than enough for

everyone!" Spartan pulled more from the racks.

"Put it on, guys, it'll keep you alive longer."

Spartan moved to the weapons rack and checked the shotguns. They were standard police issue but he was surprised to see the Kerberon Police stamps on some of them. He thought of mentioning it to the General but decided against it. Right now they had more pressing problems than where the weapons came from. They needed to fight their way to safety. Whether that was on this vessel or off somewhere else he didn't know.

"Here, take this one, you get seven shots before you need to reload," He tossed the first shotgun to the closest of the prisoners.

As the man examined the weapon Spartan pulled more of the guns down and loaded them ready for action. Although they were shotguns they still used conventional box magazines for the ammunition. He was surprised to find such a variety of ammunition types, including the full power thermal charges that were reserved for use by Special Forces or armoured tactical units. He grabbed a shotgun and three clips, throwing his carbine over to the soldier who looked amazingly happy to get his hands on a conventional firearm. With the group all armed Spartan looked over their small party. Each man wore the riot armour and carried a mixture of carbines, pistols and shotguns. It wasn't ideal but they were at the very least armed and equipped to a level that they could protect themselves.

"Follow me," said General Rivers, who then moved out into the corridor and proceeded to move along slowly. Spartan was next, his shotgun low and pointed forward, the rest followed, each of them checking behind, nervously expecting to be ambushed at any moment.

"Plan, Sir?"

"No plan, just keep moving forward till we have options."

Spartan carried on, happy with the options so far. As they reached the end of the corridor it veered off at a right angle to the right and then back to the left into what appeared to be a large open space. From their position in the corridor it wasn't entirely clear what the room was for, but their only option was to keep going towards it. Rivers moved his finger to his mouth and then moved quietly forward. He turned to the right and then left into the room. As he disappeared Spartan followed immediately behind. As Spartan emerged into the room he stopped in his tracks. Out in front it expanded into a space the size of a sports hall. Lines of cylinders in long rows ran the full length of the area. The cylinders contained a light blue fluid and from where they stood they could see dark, humanoid shapes inside each one.

"What the hell is this place?" asked General Rivers.

Spartan turned his head, he had no idea but then he spotted movement. It was the men who were questioning him before the breakout. They were standing around a panel at the far end of the room and furiously talking to someone. As Spartan watched them one saw him and called out.

"Go!" shouted Spartan and he ran in the direction of the men.

Two metal doors slid upwards and in rushed more men, some armed and a few in armour. As Spartan ran a round whistled past his head and he instinctively dropped to his knees and slid along the floor. He crashed down alongside one of the cylinders and without pausing lifted his shotgun and aimed at the newly arrived men. Two of them were clearly members of the crew as they wore overalls and carried well-worn carbines. With a single shot Spartan blasted the closest with a thermal shell. The power of the weapon was devastating and burnt its way through the man's chest and shoulder. He dropped down screaming in pain, he had only seconds left to live. More shots blasted through the hall as the prisoners scattered. Only the ex-soldier had the training and instincts to take cover and return fire. His short bursts on the carbine confirmed to Spartan that he had told the truth about being in the Army. Though Spartan was now pinned down by pistol fire he watched with satisfaction as two men tried to rush the soldier only to be cut down in a long accurate burst that struck both of the men in the face.

"Nice," whispered Spartan to himself as he readied to

do the same.

He was about to move when a loud clunk came from the cylinder he was hiding next to. With a hiss a great torrent of lukewarm liquid rushed out onto the floor and all over him. As he wiped it from his face he spotted the dark shape of whatever was inside the container. For just a second he thought it was one of the prisoners then he recognised the large, terrible form of biomechanical shock troopers he' d last seen on the surface of Proxima.

"Oh, shit!" he shouted as the thing lunged at him, slamming a moistened and dripping fist in his direction. Only Spartan's close combat experience and training could have prepared him for the speed of the attack and he avoided the first blow by just a few centimetres.

He rolled over to his side as the fighting continued on around him. From the corner of his eye he saw one of the prisoners take multiple hits from a carbine, each of the rounds opening up a bright red patch where it struck. He was unable to help though as he jumped to his feet saw the great beast in front of him. Unlike those he had fought on the colony of Avagana on Prime, this one was unprepared for military operations. It was completely naked and pale from its time inside the cylinder, for the first time he was able to see the grotesque and mutated form of the thing. At first glance it looked like something children might describe as an ogre or troll. It stood over two metres tall and its torso was wider and thicker than any man's. All of its muscles bulged with pent up power and its face was contorted and twisted into that of a brute. The neck was thickened and the mouth harder and predatory in look.

"Kill him!" One of the men near the computer displays shouted to the creature.

Spartan reached for his shotgun but the monster stamped down hard, its weight easily damaging the weapon and moving it beyond reach. Spartan looked about only to see more of the cylinders venting fluid onto the floor. General Rivers and the soldier were behind cover and still engaged in a shootout with the rest of the enemy forces. The other three ex-prisoners cowered in cover, occasionally returning fire but adding little to the battle either way. General Rivers spotted Spartan's predicament and fired a single thermal shell at the creature before being forced back into cover by a fusillade of shots.

Unlike the impact against the crewman the thermal shotgun was only able to cause superficial damage to the creature and seemed to enrage it even more. He jumped forward and delivered a series of powerful punches that slammed into the creature's ribs. Each strike felt like Spartan was hitting a punch bag yet there appeared to be little effect. He changed tack and swung his fist up into an uppercut that hit the thing in the jaw. It was like punching metal and the impact must have broken several bones in his fingers as he winced in pain.

"My turn!" the creature roared in a barely understandable

growl.

Spartan was so surprised to hear it speak that he failed to duck against the slow but powerful strike. The first hit Spartan in the chest and knocked him backwards several metres before he slumped to the ground. He felt as though his heart had stopped, the power was immense and it was incredible that the blow hadn't smashed clean through his sternum. Spartan was no weakling however and though still in pain lifted himself up, moving back to fight. The gunfire had stopped but he was unable to take his attention away from the monster. It staggered towards him, swinging its arms to catch him. This time Spartan was ready and as the strikes came in he ducked and swerved to avoid them, hitting it in the face and throat as he desperately looked for any kind of weakness.

The creature roared in anger as it missed Spartan time and time again. This time it waited and as Spartan struck it lifted its massive hands and blocked the attack, grabbing Spartan and locking his arm. It was a contest of muscle now and though Spartan was probably the toughest marine in the entire Corps he was nothing compared to this beast. He tensed his muscles, desperately trying to avoid having his arm snapped back. As this grudge match continued the creature pushed its other arm against Spartan's throat and pushed hard. The combined pressure on his arm and neck was devastating yet still Spartan refused to give in.

"Spartan, the knife!" General Rivers shouted from

somewhere in the background.

A flurry of gunshots immediately followed and then silence, just the noise of the two titans battling it out in a simple struggle of brawn. Spartan tried to remember about the knife, then recalled taking one from the room when the others took the guns. He lowered his still free left arm and felt for the knife. It was in his belt as expected, he grabbed the hilt just as his vision started to blur. Dots and speckles danced around his eyes and he knew it wouldn't be long before he would lose consciousness.

"Die!" he cried out as he used every last ounce of strength to push the arm back to give him access to the creature's face. With a single powerful thrust he stabbed upwards and into its throat and up into the brain. As soon as the blade embedded itself he felt a shudder through the creature. Its grip on Spartan loosened and he struggled free only to fall backwards onto the floor. He shook his head to see the monster falling down towards his face.

"Oh fuck!" he cried and rolled over to his right, narrowly avoiding the weighty bulk of the creature as it collapsed in a dead heap next to him. Spartan was surprised that he had actually brought down one of the monsters using just a knife and his bare hands. Then he noticed the complete lack of gunfire and could only hope it meant they had cleared the room. He stood up and looked around the open space only to find the soldier, General Rivers and one of the prisoners all with their hands on their heads and guarded by security guards. Spartan made to move towards them when he sensed something to his left. He turned to spot the great bulk of three more of the biomechanical creatures.

"You've got to be kidding me!"

With a roar the three rushed towards him and though he lifted his hands to protect his face the last thing he saw was what looked like a fleshy freight train smashing towards him. He was unconscious before his body even touched the floor.

CHAPTER THREE

The datapad and associated hardware was the brainchild of the Fairwater Corporation. Though not the more advanced hardware, it did become successful upon its introduction to the Confed military as the front end to strategic and tactical systems. The civilian models sold well due to their military credentials and though the innards constantly improved the outside appearance and functionality remained the same. The reasons for its lack of change ultimately became its reason for widespread acceptance.

Computer Science 101, 7th Edition

Teresa held her breath, her heart pounding away as she watched the burnt out wreckage of a freighter drift inch by inch past her window. According to the ship's computers this part of the debris field was supposed to be clear, but with no power being sent to the manoeuvring thrusters they had to wait and pray the ship didn't get too close. Sitting next to her were her fellow marines, Anderson and Bishop who waited in silence, each of them thinking the same as the hulks of metal followed their course. There was always the faint possibility that their calculations were wrong in some way and it was for this nightmare scenario that Commander Anderson had his hand waiting on the emergency thrust button. It would take several seconds to warm up and the boost of power would draw attention to any vessels within a day's travel. They had already been tempted to use thrust to move out of danger but that would potentially negate their mission and expose them to even more danger. They had to be patient, it was going to take an hour to slip through the debris field but it was worth it. By taking this route they had avoided the automated customs drones that patrolled the shipping lanes leading to the inner planets of Proxima.

Kowalski leaned forward. He was the resident computer and electronics expert. Thin and wiry he gave the impression of being nothing but a tech nerd. However, in their recent combat actions on the Rim had shown he could handle himself in a situation, even though he was obviously more comfortable with a computer than a rifle.

"You okay, Teresa?"

"Yeah, just thinking about Spartan and the others."

"Don't you worry about them, Marcus and Spartan

are a pair of tough bastards and General Rivers, well, you know his reputation."

Teresa did her best to smile back but it wasn't easy to hide her feelings. It felt as though her guts had been ripped out. A friendly chat or joke would do little to hide the fact that Spartan had been gone for more than two months and there were no guarantees they would ever see him again. He wasn't just her friend, they were much closer than that and if it hadn't been for the uprising on Prime and the Naval Station on the moon of Kronus they would be together right now. The more she thought of the fighting the more she started to really hate the Zealots and their self-righteous dogma that had started all the trouble in the first place.

Commander Anderson was watching the craft slip past.

"Look, can you see the markings on the side of the wreckage? That's from an old Navy cutter, you can see part of the registration mark near the burn marks."

"How did we lose a cutter out here?"

"Good question, Bishop, I haven't heard of any losses in the last few weeks. She must have been lost in counter piracy operations before the start of the uprising."

They watched the wreckage, each looking for any signs that might indicate what had caused the vessel's demise. It was like looking at a dead animal, both disturbing and also surprisingly interesting. Behind and around the craft a large amount of broken metal and debris drifted with it. As they passed through the material the tiny pieces sounded like rain on the roof of a house.

Kowalski looked over to the Commander.

"If any of that crap makes it inside the engine inlets or any of the moving parts out there you know we'll be in a world of pain, Sir?" He added the 'sir' as an afterthought.

"You'd better hope nothing gets inside then." Anderson examined the outside of their ship with the external camera mounts.

The crew was an odd little bunch. Anderson, the XO of a major capital ship had been given the use of the Tamarisk, along with the small crew, to investigate a gathering of insurgents out on the Rim. The mission had been partially successful but the information they had uncovered reached Kerberos too late to stop the coup and assassination of the President of the colony and his staff. Of that mission the four surviving marines Bishop, Teresa, Barca and Kowalski were still with him after he had requested they be assigned to his latest mission. Sadly one of the marines, a tough, burly man called Williams had been killed during their escape from the Rim. The only other member of their crew had been the Kerberon, Special Agent Johnson. He'd returned to his unit on Kerberos, though Anderson suspected that was on the orders of Naval Intelligence. The small group had bonded well since being thrown together for their first mission. Now that their new mission had been deemed critical by the Admiral of the Fleet they had an extra incentive to get the job done as quickly and efficiently as possible. It was well over a month since they'd returned after their violent escape from the Rim and their voyage home to rejoin the Fleet. The return journey itself had proven almost as epic an undertaking as the mission itself. Since their arrival back on their home ship, the CCS Santa Cruz, Teresa and the rest of the team hadn't wasted a single minute while trying to discover the location of Spartan.

So far the only clue was an audio recording handed to them by loyalists in a merchant fleet. There was no information other than that they had found the item on a transport heading from Kerberos. The destination was unknown though Teresa suspected it would be either the Rim or the inner planets, possibly Prometheus. They were the most violent and also the least policed parts of the Proxima Star System, the best places to hide all manner of goods, people and business.

As she sat there in silence she lifted up a headset and listened to the small segment of audio the technicians at Naval Intelligence had managed to salvage. At first the audio appeared to be just noise, it was more like the wind sound you could hear when lowering a window on a car. As the microphone adjusted for the ambient noise however the sound lowered until the clip became almost silent. Then the voices of three men started in low tones.

"Come on, they'll be back to check on him any second,

pass it..." said a voice before it distorted in a loud crackle.

There was a loud roaring sound as the person evidently spoke directly into the unit, before the software adjusted the recording level again to compensate.

"This is General Rivers of the Confederate Fleet. I am with Private Keller and Sergeant Spartan. Forces in collusion with the separatists have imprisoned us on Kerberos, following their assassination of the President. We are being transported to an unknown destination." Others voices then started trying to hush him.

Teresa listened closely, trying to pick out t heir voices. She had listened to the clip dozens of times but even now was finding it difficult t o pickup any of the individuals in the room. Naval Intelligence had already confirmed there were three voices, one positively identified as General Rivers. She was listening for Spartan and couldn't tell one way or the other. The voice continued.

"We have not performed planetary re-entry, I repeat, we are not on a planetary..." again the voice cut out.

A loud thud could be heard followed by shouting. Nothing intelligible could be heard though it was obvious a struggle was going on in the room or storage space that the prisoners were being held in. As the noise became louder she could hear occasional words from other people, not all were in English and some of the accents were Kerberon and Promethean. Naval Intelligence has been able to confirm the accents but not where they were being held.

Teresa concentrated even harder now and the last part, and for her the most important part, of the audio played. The sound in the room lowered, presumably because they had been overcome. Somebody must have been getting closer to the recording device.

"...will co-operate or die, the choice...fight..." and then the voice faded.

A short burst of static followed and then the file stopped.

Teresa had listened to the last line so often it felt as though it had burnt into her mind. The most important line to her though was the "co-operate or die". It was surprisingly clear and the accent was definitely from the Rim territories. Intelligence hadn't been able to identify the individual speaking but they had done the next best thing, they had found the man's voice on other recordings taken from surveillance the previous year during a narcotics operation. The group had been broken up but it was known they were still running guns from Kerberos to Prime where their weapons had been used in the insurgency and eventually the mass uprising.

It didn't matter to Teresa though what had happened, all she wanted to know was where they were and more importantly to her, where Spartan was. She hadn't realised how important he was to her until the news had hit her on his arrest and then sudden disappearance. She had decided weeks ago that being reunited with Spartan was her single goal and she would not stop until she had him back. If that meant going against the Fleet's orders, so be it. Luckily for them all, the mission they were on had so far proved compatible.

The latest information had suggested that a weapons trade would be conducted anytime in the next twenty-four hours and this point was a strong candidate for the loading of the goods. The debris field followed a steady orbit around the burning star but of more importance to traders and dealers it provided an unlimited source of hiding places. Their current course would take them directly to a recently used drop off point platform, a small but spacious manmade station about a hundred metres in diameter and perfect for storing goods to be collected by a buyer. There were hundreds of similar storage spots, many more out on the Rim, but intelligence confirmed that members of the group associated with who had taken General Rivers and his team were supposed to be heading this way.

To maintain the element of surprise they had to slip into the area avoiding all manner of black market dealers and pirates. Their ship was after all only a heavily modified cargo hauler, not a ship of war. It had taken them over a week to get into position in this treacherous area without using the main shipping lanes. The only chance they had of reaching the small drop off platform, without alerting the many spies loyal to the separatists, was to slip past the security patrols with no running engines and most of their systems offline.

The great hulk of the derelict craft continued to tumble its way past them, though from where they sat its course appeared to take a lifetime. Anderson watched it move along the thick, reinforced window before it continued on to the left of the ship. As it moved to a safe distance the crew breathed a sigh of relief.

"Bloody hell, that was close."

"You don't say, Bishop. Are we likely to run into more derelicts on this route?"

Bishop pulled up a navigation chart on the computer system and rechecked their position.

"Well, Sir, we've managed to avoid the main shipping lanes for the last week. We should drift into position about five hundred kilometres from the drop-off platform. Assuming we make it that close without being detected, we should be able to land a boarding party via the shuttle before they can get their people onto their ships and away."

A red light started to flash on the tactical display, shortly followed by a low tone.

"What the hell?" Teresa muttered.

"Sir, we've got trouble. I'm picking up two vessels, ten kilometres out and moving fast," said Bishop.

"Have they spotted us?" asked Commander Anderson, the senior ranking member of the crew and leader of their operation.

Bishop clicked his fingers to get the attention of Kowalski who was already scanning the electronic signals emanating from the approaching craft.

"I'm on it!"

He flicked between each page of data, checking for their power levels and readiness of weapon systems. From the look on his face he looked less than happy.

"This isn't good, this isn't good at all. The sensors show the transport is prepping a shuttle. There's a lot of activity coming from inside, I'd say there are a number of people on board and they are getting ready for something. No major power systems switching on, doesn't mean they won't have projectile weapons already loaded and waiting though."

He then brought up a detailed schematic of a civilian ship. It rotated about on the screen and several pages of data and specifications scrolled upwards. Kowalski read a few lines before turning to the rest of the crew.

"Right, I've got the ship's specs. She is a Centaur Class transport. A light hauler used mainly on the shipping runs from the Rim to the refineries and industrial colonies. According to the data she has a crew of three and can transport up to a dozen passengers plus assorted cargo. The other vessel has the same electronic signature but there's a lot of interference coming from her engineering coils. Either she's damaged or her power plant has been upgraded in some way."

"Engines? Maybe it's a modified version, like a tug?" Bishop suggested.

"That isn't really necessary though, unless she's been altered with more substantial manoeuvring thrusters of course. Either way we'll find out soon enough, the transport is moving into a position alongside us. They'll be here in less than two minutes!"

The public wideband channel on the emergency communications panel flashed to show an unencrypted transmission had been picked up on the emergency transponder. Without intervention the equipment transferred the data to the screen. At first is showed a simple arrangement of coloured bars before fading away to show a man's face. It was a one-way signal, presumably from the approaching vessels and didn't use the normal communications system present on board the Tamarisk.

"This is Ramillies, your transport is encroaching on a private meeting. We can only assume your intentions are hostile. Open your cargo bays for inspection and prepare to be boarded, resistance will be met with accordingly."

Commander Anderson gave the screens a quick look before turning to his small crew. His face showed concern but he was far from panicked.

"They aren't coming to inspect us, if they knew who we were though they'd already be shooting. I've seen the reports on these groups in this area. You've seen the wreckage of the cutter as well. They seize the ship and tow it to the nearest yard where they strip the tech, move the goods and then usually kill the crew. If you're lucky you get sent off to the slavers on the Rim or Prometheus. The carcass of the your ship will then either but towed away for scrap or if it is a military vessel they usually dump it."

"Bullshit, they're not taking us!"

"I never suggested otherwise, Teresa. I don't think any of us is in the mood to just hand over such a sweet ship as ours," he said with a wicked smile.

Barca, who until then had been silent, joined in. "Now we find out if those modifications are worth the effort the tech guys put into them."

He was the shortest of the marines, with the exception of Teresa, but had the broad build and attitude of a man who had been bullied and harassed over the years for his size. After several years service in the Marine Corps he was as tough as they came, even if that came at the price of his less than inspiring social skills.

"Bishop, get on the weapons platform and make sure you're ready. Barca! Teresa! Break out the weapons and then get down to the hangar bay. If any of them manage to get inside it's your job to make sure they get no further. There are carbines and thermal shotguns on the rack, you know where they are."

Teresa nodded and immediately started to untie herself from her position in front of the computer system. As she extricated herself Commander Anderson then turned to Kowalski.

"Can you jam their transmissions once the shooting starts? If we lose our cover we might as well have not bothered coming here."

"Can do, Sir, when we get within one hundred metres I'll drop a dampening net in this section. Nothing will get in or out until we power down the field. There is a problem though, the kind of power we'll be putting out will make us stick out to any other vessels in this area. If they have friends they'll be onto us in minutes."

"Perhaps, but once the shooting starts that will happen anyway. The trick is to keep it short, fast and violent."

Kowalski snorted to himself, "Fast and violent huh? That's my speciality!"

He shouted after Bishop who was already pulling himself along the inside of the ship towards the weapon control console that was a few metres further back in the habitation section.

"Bishop, do not under any circumstances start the targeting matrix up until I give you the word. Once they know we are armed and ready they'll know the game is up."

"Yeah, yeah, it's not my first time, Kowalski."

He pulled himself over to the weapon control system and strapped himself into the chair. Directly in front were a dozen screens as well as the manual overrides for the mechanical weapon systems. Though the Tamarisk was a civilian transport she had been heavily modified into what was known as a 'Q' ship. By removing sections of the cargo areas a variety of weapon systems had been fitted. Hinged plates and shutters covered the weapons and the additional armour that had also been installed. The middle part of the vessel, and by far the largest, was the central spine onto which six large containers ran lengthwise along a hexagonal joint. From the front it looked like the ship was almost cylindrical due to the containers that were fitted to the top, bottom and sides. The containers were the parts of the ship that had been modified the most, though from the outside she just looked like an old, slightly out of date haulage vessel. In reality she had the firepower to take on a ship of the same size, possibly even larger, even more importantly she had surprise on her side. At least, that is what they hoped.

"Sixty seconds, Commander," said Kowalski, his voice slightly higher pitched than before.

Barca and Teresa were at the main sealed bulkhead doorway that led into the cargo area. They were both wearing their work suits, much like the PDS armoured suits used by the marines but less sophisticated and lacking the communication equipment and defences of the military. The suits were equipped with mounts for a variety of tools, the exteriors of both were well worn and pockmarked with dents and scratches. They had originally been a dark red colour but over time had faded and several repair patches did nothing to enhance the looks of the gear. In reality they were extremely well maintained but to the untrained eye they were industrial and outdated compared to the more recent suits and body armour. Neither of them were wearing helmets, though Teresa was already removing one from the wall mount and Barca was busy checking the seals on his own before he pulled the helmet down onto his head. When on the ship it was fine to have the external automatic visor in the upright position. This just left the reinforced glass visor fixed in place to maintain a full sealed environment in the suit.

Taking some effort they unlocked the sealed section and then pulled their weightless bodies inside the internal spine of the ship. It was several metres wide, easily large enough for the two of them, and ran the entire length of the ship. As they moved down it they they passed the first entry section where a doorway led into each of the containers. The doors formed a hexagonal ring and they were all sealed with traditional wheeled seals. These ships could carry all manner of containers and equipment, so it was imperative that the connections between the ship and the cargo were both strong and sealed. The worst fear on any of these vessels was that of opening a hatch to find nothing but the void and a painful death on the other side.

Teresa called to Barca, "Get weapons. We'll cover the corridors from behind those storage lockers."

Just inside the shaft was a locked cabinet which she quickly opened to reveal a weapon rack containing a dozen weapons. Most were ultra low calibre pistols for use on ships, but there was also a modified thermal shotgun and an unusual riot carbine with built in shotgun slung under the main barrel. It had been important from the start that they carried only weapons ever used on the civilian market or likely to have been purchased on the black market. Having a ship full of L48 rifles or carbines would be an easy giveaway that they were a marine party.

Barca leaned forward and grabbed the shotgun and then one of the pistols that he then stuffed into his belt. As Teresa took her own set of weapons a series of clunks rattled through the hardened metal of the ship. Barca looked to Teresa who was busy checking the carbine.

"What the hell is that?"

"Sounds like the container motors starting up, they'll be needed to open the flaps to the weapon systems."

A low whine came from the wall as the internal speaker system activated.

"They are approaching on the port side. I'm opening the clear containers for them to inspect. The armed units will stay closed for the next thirty seconds," came the familiar voice of Bishop who was still manning the weapon controls.

"Anderson here. Remember the plan. When I give the order we hit the dampening field. With their signals jammed we will have a small window. Kowalski estimates we will have about thirty seconds, forty top, before they can power up and get far enough away to burn through our blocks with their transmissions. If they can get away from us the mission will be exposed and we'll be back to square one. Bishop will eliminate the engines on both craft with the first volleys of fire. Assuming we succeed we'll proceed with the capture of their ships. Minimise casualties, we need prisoners and intel. Don't kill them and don't destroy the ships. That goes for you especially, Barca. Capture, don't destroy!"

Barca looked over to Teresa and grinned before pulling down the darkened visor on his helmet. Much like a welding mask the helmet visor could adjust to all levels of light, making them perfect for welding work or accidental exposure to the full burning glare of the sun. They were now both fully equipped, ready for battle and potentially for extra vehicular activity (EVA), movement outside the ship in the vacuum of space. With a final check on the internal doors they moved back and took up positions behind cover, planting their feet inside the railing to anchor themselves down. From this position they had a full arc of fire that covered the entire length of the spine. If anybody managed to board through the cargo or engine areas they would have to pass through this corridor.

Teresa tapped a button on the wall to activate the ship's internal communications system.

"We're in position, the spine is secured and the doors are locked down. We're ready!"

Bishop and Kowalski both turned and looked towards Commander Anderson for the final word on the operation. He in turn looked back and double-checked the range to the approaching craft.

"Okay, Kowalski, you have the numbers, as soon as they hit the marker you release the field and then help Bishop with the weapons. Ready?"

Both marines nodded before turning back to their view screens.

"Okay, both vessels are coming into range in 5...4...3...2...1," he said as calmly as possible.

On the screen the tug had changed course slightly and was moving above the crew area at a slow crawl. The transport craft however was in place directly parallel with the Tamarisk and her cargo doors were already starting to open.

"Here goes nothing!" cried Kowalski as he hit the release button.

A low buzz travelled through the ship as the modified dampening field fitted by the Naval engineers powered up and then released its electronic screen. There was nothing to actually see but Tamarisk's own sensors and diagnostic screen indicated a block to all data transmission and reception, as well as communication on anything other than hard wired data lines. Kowalski did a quick wide band check and immediately found attempts to transmit from the enemy craft.

"Okay, they're blocked, do your work!"

Bishop triggered the unlock mechanism, clunks and shudders travelled through the great hulk of the ship. From the outside it looked simply like more of the cargo doors were opening. There was a good chance that the hostile vessels' own crews would be more confused than anything else. With their systems jammed it could easily be solar disruption or equipment failure. It wouldn't matter anyway. As soon as the weapons opened fire it would be clear what was happening.

"Dragging out the guns!" Bishop shouted as he hit the ready button.

In four of the containers sat pairs of 40mm flak guns. These ancient relics from the early Navy warships were the least advanced weaponry in the Fleet. In fact they would have been equally at home on board ocean-based shipping in the twentieth century. The only concession to later designs was that they were all equipped with auto-loading hardware and gyroscopic motorised mounts. Once the doors were fully open the pairs of guns moved forward two metres so that the barrels protruded from the containers like a series of radio masts. The barrels of each weapon were over a metre long and the ammunition boxes were packed with both armour-piercing and high explosive rounds, each selectable via the weapon control systems inside the ship.

On the tactical display Bishop had two targeting patterns already loaded in. The guns in three of the four containers had a direct line of sight to the targets and in less than two seconds had pivoted into position and loaded armour-piercing rounds. The high explosives might do better against these kinds of lighter armed vessels but they wanted prisoners, not destruction.

Commander Anderson watched over the unfolding drama and spotted the manoeuvring thrusters already adjusting on the tug. So far they still had the element of surprise. He took a deep breath.

"Fire!"

Bishop, on hearing the order hit the button for the firing pattern to commence. The vibration rippled through the ship as the large weapons opened fire. On the bridge of the Tamarisk Commander Anderson had a perfect view of the approaching vessel. It was positioned about a hundred metres off the port side and a dozen 40mm shells had already struck the engines and after section. Sparks and flashes scattered along the rear of the ship and at least one round must have struck a fuel or chemical tank as a blinding flash tore out a large chunk and split it in two.

"Holy shit!" swore Bishop as he watched the screen.

The guns fell silent on the flank only for the weapons to pivot around and join in with the other four guns already blazing away at the tug. Either the craft was extremely lucky or it was equipped with additional armour as after sustaining over a hundred rounds it was still intact and its engines were starting to light up.

"Bishop!"

"I'm on it, Sir!" Bishop ran his fingers over the control systems for the weapons. He made minor modifications and set one of the guns to fire a series of high explosive rounds. With a short burst of clattering fire another thirty shells ripped through the craft on its engines all along the hull. As sparks and flashes danced about on the screen he noticed a hatch opening on the underside of the craft. As he zoomed in the colour literally drained from his face.

"That's no tug, look!" he called as he sent the video feed to the other displays.

Before any of them had anything to add a series of blue muzzle flashes appeared from the hatch. The internal alarms responded instantly as a dozen holes appeared in the hull of the Tamarisk. Both vessels continued to rake each other with fire as they stood off at short distance.

"We're taking damage throughout container four and the sleeping quarters have been breached," said Kowalski as he checked the status of all sections of the ship. "I've lost control of half the guns, they must have cut through the control units after one of the first hatches."

Commander Anderson poured over the schematics of their ship before spotting the point Kowalski was referring to. It was a large armoured control unit mounted in the spine of the ship, deep behind armour and the protection of the containers.

"What the hell? That's where Teresa is." He grabbed the intercom.

A loud crash came from inside the ship and a series of flashes and sparks raced across the computer displays.

"Commander, they are in two of the containers!" Teresa's voice was cut off by the sound of gunfire.

Another massive volley from the Tamarisk finally cut its way through the hull armour of the tug vessel and a small explosion must have cut her power as the ship went dark, its weapons either destroyed or offline. Either way, both of the enemy ships were drifting without power and they appeared defenceless.

"Bishop, get down there and give them a hand, we can't let them get inside, one thermal charge and we're screwed!"

"Yes, Sir!" There wasn't a moment's pause as Bishop tore off his harness and pulled down his helmet from the mount next to the display. Clicking it into place he pushed off and moved back towards the hatch leading down to the spine. He didn't bother grabbing a weapon as he was already wearing a C9 automag in his thigh holster, a common black market weapon that was available at almost every station and platform in the Confederacy. He undid the seal and pulled open the hatch that led directly into the airlock section, the final divider between the crew and passenger section and the cargo and transport part of the ship. As the door closed behind him the hatch in front opened up to a blazing firefight between Barca and Teresa and a number of armoured men. He was forced to pull himself out of the way as a series of low velocity slugs pattered away at the door.

"Get out of the way!" shouted Teresa who was busy blasting away from behind the pockmarked cover she had set up.

He pulled himself up against the wall and looked along the corridor to the sight of five men, all in military issue body armour. It was the old specification carapace system that fifty years ago was the standard gear used by marines and soldiers in the armed forces. It was much thicker and more cumbersome than the PDS now used. In many ways it was better suited to large-scale ground warfare with its greater resilience to weapon fire and fragmentation. There were still some units being equipped to reserve units in the army, though the marines had phased out using them.

Bishop pulled out his automag and flicked the catch to ready it for combat. Unlike most of the weapons now used it still used a manual bolt and firing pin system like twenty-first century weapons. Aiming carefully he pointing it at the two men who had just climbed out of the container hatch. The first looked back and quickly moved out of the way fire. Barca pushed himself up adjusting his position so that he could bring down fire onto the head of the nearest man. He pulled the trigger releasing a long burst of fire that was so fast it sounded like a zip being undone. It wasn't as powerful as the military grade weapons they were used to, but the sheer weight of fire caught both men and knocked them back. As one struck the wall he lost his grip on his rifle and tumbled back into the open space in the corridor. The second man tried to hang on but ended up spinning around. Not wanting to miss the opportunity Teresa leaned out from her cover and took careful aim with the riot carbine. She pulled the secondary trigger and sent a blast of superheated thermal pellets. The whole group were struck by the blast though no major injuries or damage were caused. In the confusion of the blast she pulled the primary trigger and released a three round burst hitting the closest man's hand. Additional bursts struck both men across their bodies and one in the head. In just a few seconds they were both dead. The other three made a desperate rush to the rear of the vessel to try and escape from the gunfire.

"They're going for our power plant, put them down!" shouted Barca and he jumped in after them.

"Barca, get back!" Teresa shouted as she fired more shots. Unfortunately because Barca had moved ahead he was now blocking the line of sight. One of the enemy had spotted this and turned back to fire a burst from his rifle. Most of the rounds clattered harmlessly into the thick skin of the ship but three managed to reach Barca, two hit the think armour on his arm but one found the glass visor and easily smashed inside, striking him in the face. His suit instantly depressurised and he drifted lifelessly where he fell.

"Bastards!"

Teresa slammed in another clip and emptied the entire set of rounds. Bishop moved forward and added his own fire as he pulled Barca's unmoving body down to safety. Several of the incoming rounds struck Barca's amour, giving Bishop the time and cover he needed to reload and fire a final burst until just one of the enemy remained. He was busy trying to connect a device to the panel at the end of the corridor. Bishop fired a single round above the man's head.

"Hey, your buddies are gone. Hands up or eat a bullet!"

Teresa pulled herself along, holding her pistol out in front as she approached the man. As she moved closer she could see that he hadn't brought a weapon on board, it was a computerised hacking unit designed to gain entry into their computer system and give them control over the ship. The man turned around and lifted his hands. As he released the unit it drifted away and clattered against the wall of the corridor.

"We're clear down here, and we have a prisoner, Sir."

"Good work, Teresa, any casualties?"

Teresa looked back towards Bishop who was checking Barca. She could see that he wasn't coming back though.

The visor on the suits had limited protection against debris but against firearms it was almost unless.

"Yes, Sir, Barca is dead, he was killed in the firefight."

There was a short pause.

"How about the prisoner?"

Teresa looked back at the man in the carapace armour. Through the thickened glass she could see the fear in his eyes.

"Why are you on my ship?"

"I..uh...I..." he muttered in confusion.

Teresa turned her head slightly and raised her pistol so that it was just a few centimetres from his face.

"I asked you a question!"

"We are looking for strays to sell."

"To sell? Who to?"

The man was taking no chances now and answered immediately.

"Slavers, they are paying ten times over the going rate for some big project," he said, desperately trying to appease her as she maintained the position of the weapon in front of his face.

CHAPTER FOUR

Alpha Company was one of the first companies to establish a permanent paramilitary training facility on Terra Nova. The well trained personnel were often members of the Army or Marine Corps and provided bodyguards and security staff for some of the most important companies in the Confederacy. Their claim to fame being, that they were the first private corporation to finance and build their own cruiser. With its range of firepower and ability to project power they quickly became the number one security company in the System.

Private Security Directory

The manacles on his hands and feet were impossible to remove. Spartan had been wriggling and tugging for the last hour and so far the only result had been a new series of cuts and bruises on his limbs. With a final effort he stopped and looked about the room. It was the same cell he had been in earlier but the numbers of prisoners had been reduced. General Rivers must have been taken somewhere else, along with the other escapees, as there was no sign of him. He did notice that Marcus was still in the room and it didn't looked like he was starting to regain consciousness. The door was locked and he hadn't seen anybody for almost three hours now. The temptation to try and escape when they were taken to the lavatory was always there. But since his attempted escape all prisoners, when taken out of the room, were escorted by six fully armoured guards.

He thought back to the violent battle during their escape and the large room. His memory of the event was still a little hazy, no doubt due to the abuse he took at the hands of the enemy. A few key images did stick in his mind though. The cylinders were full of fluid, he was certain of that, as the nearest one had dumped gallons of the stuff all over his body.

What really interested him though was the image of the creature staggering out and attacking him. It was the only time he had seen one out of its customary armour and what he had seen definitely convinced him that they were human, or at least part human. Contrary to what some had told him, they were certainly not machines, no more than any living thing wasn't a machine. There was something else though, what was it? Then he remembered. The creature had spoken to him. This was the only instance he had heard anything other than grunts or roaring sounds from the creatures. The ability to speak immediately moved it out of the machine or creature camp and into a human of some kind.

The next question was what were the cylinders and fluids all about? There could only be a few reasons for them being like that, though he was hardly a scientist. It could be a way of transporting the creatures from place to place. The liquid might be a way of regenerating damaged tissue or to provide a cushion during high-speed travel. That was hardly likely though, they were tough and easily able to be strapped into place prior to high acceleration. Maybe it was something else. The creature was unarmoured, and nowhere as potent in hand-to-hand combat as ones he'd faced in battle before. Maybe they were newly born or perhaps even infants? After all, they had to be born, modified or created somehow and the cylinders might have something to do with it.

As he lay there, chained like a common criminal, he heard a series of loud thumping sounds pounding through the hull. They became louder until he could feel the vibrations through the floor. Two of the prisoners started moaning at the sound.

"What is it?" His immediate thoughts were that it must be related to the great creatures further along in the ship.

"It's the ship, they are making adjustments before the

shielding, we must be entering a storm area," said one of the prisoners.

Spartan was surprised at finding a man with any kind of starship knowledge on board. Only somebody with transport knowledge or engineering know-how could surely understand that kind of thing. Though the more he thought about it the more he realised it was stupid to think otherwise. So far he had found prisoners from all walks of life.

"How do you know that?"

"I've spent my time on freighters, trust me, they are changing the makeup of the plating and electrical shielding. They only do this when they know they are going to hit a danger zone. If I had to guess I'd say we must be heading to Prometheus."

"Prometheus?"

"Yeah, you heard of the place?"

Spartan said nothing for a moment as he thought back to Prometheus. He had spent some time, prior to joining the Marine Corps, as a pit fighter in that hellhole. It was an odd place, unlike Prime or Kerberos there wasn't a central colony. The planet was a burning hot rocky ball of minerals that made habitable colonies out of the question. The only structures on the surface were those of the hundreds of mining, research and refinery operations. Even though the temperatures made engineering projects expensive and dangerous there were many benefits to working there, the primary one as always being money. Around the planet were hundreds of starbases, mining outposts, trading stations and research labs. In the middle of this mass of humanity were three military compounds including a small naval station and shipyard, an orbital Marine Corps barracks and a well-guarded research station. It was like the Wild West back on old Earth where prospectors came to make money and gamble it away on the many vices the stations had to offer.

The attraction of quick money and even quicker ways to spend it also provided the Marine Corps a suitable recruiting ground for fresh warriors. Not that Spartan had ever looked for enlistment. That came down to the police raid and subsequent accident. The look on the judge's face as he gave him the choice, prison or military service still haunted him. As he sat in chains and was heading off to yet another uncertain fate, he started to wonder once again if he had the made the right decision.

There was something that didn't make sense though. He had made the trip several times to and from Prometheus and the storms were only a problem if you went through them, but they were avoidable. It just increased the trip from days to months.

"Why though?"

"Only reason I can think of is they are going to try to sprint through the storms. Fat lot of good the shielding will do for them though, if they are hit going through the ship is toast. Actually, technically we will be toast, the ship will probably be okay."

Spartan looked less than impressed.

"What's the point of the shielding if it doesn't work then?"

"Most ships can travel fully automated. If you send her through, the shielding should be enough to protect the hardened computer systems. Biological matter though, that's something else!"

* * *

Teresa moved about inside the enemy ship. It was of a similar size to the Tamarisk and so far she had already found a dozen weapons plus secure datapads and backup drives. Bishop was in the aft of the vessel while she rummaged around in the crew areas for any information that might be of use. Both wore their suits, as they had needed to make the short EVA manoeuver between the vessels so that they could board her. As she opened one of the crew lockers the intercom in her helmet activated.

"Kowalski here. Anderson has information from the prisoner on the location of the ship's log files and communications backup. He says to go the waste disposal unit. It's two doors back from the bridge. Open the door and look to the left, you should see a set of circular doors. Open them and you'll find the data storage segment of the ship."

"In the toilet?" she asked scornfully.

"Hey, don't blame the messenger! I guess they thought it would be more secure hidden somewhere you wouldn't expect."

"They got that part right. I'm on my way, any other information?"

She moved away from the lockers and pulled her body along by holding onto the handles along the walls. The crew area was surprisingly barren though, unlike the storage area that was loaded with all kinds of air sealed containers. She moved past one metal door until she rounded a corner and could see the entrance to the bridge. Counting along the wall she spotted the correct door.

"Nothing yet, apparently this guy is ready to spill his guts though. By the time the Commander is done he won't have any secrets!"

"Good, these bottom feeders deserve everything they get!"

Pushing out her right hand she held onto the railing with her left and twisted the wheel to open the door to the waste disposal area. As it swung open she thought it was the wrong place before realising she was looking at loose plastic drapes that she had to pull through to reach the inside.

"Left, right, no…left," she muttered to herself as she felt for the door. She quickly found it and swung open the door to reveal an entire panel of glowing lights.

"Jackpot!"

"I think the Commander is going to like this!"

* * *

The lights flickered and in one final flash the room changed from pitch black into harsh white light. As Spartan lifted his manacled hand to the light a group of the familiar armoured soldiers arrived and started to unlock the chains from the wall, taking the prisoners one at a time down the hall. As Spartan watched his thoughts returned to the idea of escaping. They must have arrived at their destination, these guards were not people he had seen before and they wore patches from some kind of private security company. The patch looked a bit like a snake but he was too far away to read the lettering. Another two people were taken away and that meant Spartan was next. As three guards approached he tensed up, readying himself for any opportunity he might find. Only one guard stepped forward though, the other two lowered their thermal shotgun and aimed them at his chest. The third moved forward with a metal rod about a metre long. Spartan tried to struggle but the chains gave him just a few centimetres movement.

"Don't struggle, we're just attaching the rod!"

It didn't matter either way as the man aimed the rod at

the collar around Spartan's neck and pushed it into a notch that locked into place. As it joined together Spartan could feel it tighten around his neck, they were obviously taking no chances.

"Good, now stay calm and come with us. If you struggle this will happen..."

Spartan's eyesight blurred for a moment before he felt a sizzling fire sensation. A series of pulsing muscle spasms ripped through his body and he felt as though his spine would snap from the involuntary movements.

"The control rod will send the pulses into your spine, too much will cripple you. Understood?"

Spartan, now barely able to stand properly said nothing, his lack of defiance gave them all the encouragement they needed. The man led the chained and collared Spartan out of the room to follow the line of prisoners and guards away from his previous prison. They moved past where earlier they had stolen the weapons and armour. The burn marks on the walls had been covered up and the door and locks looked as though they had been replaced with new ones of much sturdier construction. He looked in through the thickened glass window of the small barracks room before he felt pressure on his neck.

"Move it!" shouted the man.

Spartan stumbled forward and soon reached the turn where his small group had prepared for their rush into the next section where the cylinders were fitted. The thought of seeing the mysterious part of the ship placated him for a moment and in just seconds the long column of lumbering people wandered into the open area. Spartan choked with surprise as he witnessed the shocking display. As he stared with wide eyes they all slowed down due to the congestion. It gave him a moment to survey the scene before him.

The first thing that was obvious was that the area had been cleaned up and repaired. No longer was there liquid, broken Plexiglas or the rubble of battle. The floor had been scrubbed and all the cylinders removed. In their place were a dozen of the shock troopers. Each of them stood to attention as if waiting for something. Unlike the ones he had fought before these were clothed and equipped in grapheme-based armour. The thin skin of the grapheme material was harder and stronger than steel and protected all the key body parts of the creatures without impeding their movement. Under the armour each of them wore a skin-tight suit of an unknown construction so that no skin was exposed. Their heads were all covered in a form of modified PDS helmet that had been expanded to fit the larger proportions of the monsters.

"What the hell are those things?" shouted one of the prisoners.

The man that had told Spartan about the storms and the ship's shielding turned around to whisper to him.

"I thought we'd stopped using mechanoids centuries

ago?" he said before being struck in the back by one of the guards.

It was true, Spartan had read a few accounts of the use of mechanical slave labour in the files on board the Santa Maria before his first action on Kronus. The idea of robotic machines that could move and carry out the same functions of humans had fascinated him. His interest wasn't shared though and it was well known that their use had created resentment and hostility to mechanoids that took away the livelihood of citizens. It must have been a long time ago though, well before the Great War, perhaps even before the founding of the colonies in Proxima. The machine smashing holidays were still carried out at special festivals on some of the colonial worlds in much the same way as the piñata at children's parties that were held by some families on Kerberos.

The group started to move forward and for the first time Spartan was able to see the corridors that led away from the open space and into a loading area on the ship. The prisoners were all being lined up and Spartan was surprised to see more prisoners coming in similar columns from other parts of the ship. As he turned to look back towards the shock troopers he noticed the familiar shapes of General Rivers and Marcus in the group. Marcus nodded at spotting him but none of the three did anything to get the attention of the guards. Spartan was just happy to see that his comrades were still alive after their escape debacle. The nearest guard pushed Spartan to get his attention, presumably thinking the massive hulk of the shock troopers fascinated him.

"Yeah, don't worry, son. You'll be really comfortable with the idea of those guys soon enough!" The guard started to laugh. It didn't take long for several of the other armoured men to join in.

The door at the side of the ship started to open, lifting up slowly to reveal a glass covered walkway that led inside an industrial looking complex. The open space was easily twenty metres wide and bore the faded marking of Pro-Gen, an old research company that had famously gone bust in a drug scandal about a decade earlier. It wasn't much but it did confirm two things to Spartan. First, the company facility was based on the planet of Prometheus, as expected. Second, there was a link between the shock troopers and Prometheus, though whether it was down to their training or creation remained to be seen. Along both sides of the open area stood armed guards, each with the same insignia he had seen earlier. They were all armed with shotguns, carbines and in one case some kind of heavy glaive.

From the darkness at the end of the walkway a group of men in suits approached. As they came closer Spartan noticed one man was being followed by another small group of guards, though these were carrying axes and cutlass type blades. Along with this group another of the shock troopers approached, this one carried a savage looking curved blade in one hand. It was almost as though they were back at the Siege of New Carlos though this time there were no marines and no battle.

The men stopped a short distance from the prisoners and the guards following them fanned out to provide a continuous security line back into the complex. Something clicked on Spartan's back and he found he could move more freely. Turning around he could see the guard with the rod had disconnected it from him so that only the manacles around his hands remained. He indicated for Spartan to step forward and onto the platform. As he did so many more of the prisoners stepped forward to join him. The man with his own guards seemed to be in charge. He lifted his hand, not that it was needed as the prisoners were already silent.

"I am Governor Richards, welcome to my facility. On this station we accept criminal elements from all colonies whether they are Confederate, independent or private. Soon you will join others in the secure wing where you will assist in the engineering projects we are working on as part of your sentence. Any attempts to escape will be dealt with by exposure to the planetary surface. For those of you unfamiliar with Prometheus, you will last no longer than thirty seconds in the extreme heat. There is no escape from this facility, only death, or the end of your sentence. You will choose which comes first. The rules are simple, disregard them and the punishment will be severe."

He paused for a moment and scanned the prisoners before indicating to the guards to push them forwards.

"Follow my men, they will escort you to your new home. Remember, do as you're told and you will find us fair." His was suddenly cut off. Two prisoners rushed forward along the platform and away from the ship. Spartan watched them move and for a second considered joining them, it was pointless though. They were running towards the enemy, not to safety. Before they even reached the first door the lone shock trooper blocked their path. Spartan knew they had no chance, it would take a whole marine squad or at least some heavy weapons to bring one down. As the first man staggered past it swung its left arm and struck him low in the body. It was as though the poor man had run headlong into a metal barrier. Before he had hit the ground the creature slashed at the second with its curved blade, the impact was fast and powerful and cut down through the man's collar and down to his thigh. The bloodied ruins of the man dropped into a dead heap on the ground.

"As I said. Break the rules and the punishment will be severe." The Governor indicated to the guards to grab the surviving prisoner and take to one of the small sealed doorways that led to an airlock seal. Some of the prisoners started to fidget and there was an obvious feeling of heightened tension. Spartan wasn't stupid though and it was obvious that any attempt to escape or to help this one man would end with him joining his fate.

The guards moved him up to the doorway and hit the button to the side. The door slid up revealing an airlock loading station about ten metres long that led out towards another similar doorway. The man turned around and faced the prisoners. As he started to shout the door slid down, instantly locking him into the small room.

"Now, if anybody else has the urge to break the rules you will suffer the exact same fate as this unfortunate individual. I never make threats at this facility, I only make promises."

He signalled the guards and without even pausing the first man hit the release button. The exterior door opened sending the poor man to the burning hot conditions on the surface of the planet. There was no breathable atmosphere and the heat started to burn him from the moment the door opened. The change in pressure blew him out so that he was ejected onto the burning hot surface. His clothes were on fire and his skin peeling away in just seconds. In less than a minute he was motionless and his body, still burning, sent shivers through the assembled prisoners. There was total silence in the open space and with the doors shut not a sound entered the building from the howling winds outside. Spartan glanced to his side, spotting the large, dark figure of Marcus watching the burnt husk of a man. To the casual eye he looked dispassionate but Spartan knew the man well by now and his rage was barely contained.

The Governor turned away to walk along the open space to the open doors that led into the dark caverns of the base. As he reached them something bumped into Spartan. He turned around to find the mass of prisoners pushing forward, herded like cattle along the platform to follow the Governor. Along the sides and at the front the heavily armed guards kept a watchful eye over them. He hadn't spotted it at first but as they moved through the doors a number of discreet domes protruded from the ceiling at irregular intervals. The Governor stood waiting between two of the domes about ten metres from the prisoners. He lifted his hand for them to stop.

"These domes are here for all of our protection. They are part of the automated defence system in this facility and scan all entry and exit points. Any unauthorised access by prisoners or staff will be met by these..." He pointed at the domes.

In perfect synchronisation a short barrel pushed out from the dome along with what looked like a single glowing red eye. The entire dome rotated so that the eye could view a complete 360° arc. Every few moments it stopped and the lens made an almost silent noise as it moved forwards to alter it focus, at least that is how it looked.

"Intruder detected. Return to your holding area, you have five seconds before lethal force is authorised," came an automated voice directly from the unit.

The Governor pulled a small device from his pocket and pressed a button. The red light switched off and the unit retracted back inside the dome.

"These units are everywhere on the site. If one tells you to move you had better do it fast. In the last eighty days we have had thirteen attempted escapes and one hostage taken. Every single person involved has been terminated by the sentry system. Listen to the Eye and do exactly as it tells you!"

Satisfied that the prisoners had heard his message he beckoned for one of the guards to approach. He moved forward and clicked his feet smartly.

"Sir."

"Take them to their quarters and introduce them to their duties." The Governor promptly turned and disappeared off into the blackness.

The guard cleared his throat before addressing the prisoners.

"You will follow me to your wing, a lovely new structure built by the loving hands of your predecessors. Now... follow me!" He turned towards a narrow corridor to the right. As he moved forwards the lights flickered on to bathe the area in a bright white light.

As Spartan moved forward there was only one thing on his mind. It wasn't the quarters, their jobs or even the terrible fate that awaited them all. It was plain and simple, he was thinking of the trigger device held by the Governor.

* * *

Admiral Jarvis, the senior Confederate Commander in the Proxima System stepped carefully over the cables and tools that lay strewn across the floor. To her side stood the imposing figure of Lieutenant Colonel Blake, the Commander of the 5th Reconnaissance Battalion and the senior Marine Commander from the Santa Cruz. His ship had returned from Kerberos two weeks earlier and a large number of his marines were already on the station and assisting with the defences and getting the systems up and running.

Admiral Jarvis had been on the moon of Kronus for over an hour now to survey the repair work on the Titan Naval Station and assess its readiness in case of further emergencies. As she walked through the station she was surprised to see a number of the weapon systems had been remounted and showed as live. Behind her and the Colonel were a small group of marines, each of them in their standard Personal Defence Suits (PDS) and armed with L48 rifles. They were covered from head to toe in the sealed tactical armour and were marching smartly behind her in a small column. They had been handpicked from the men and women of the Reconnaissance Battalion, the elite unit of the Marine Corps units currently in the System. Though they marched with precision they were by no means operating as just a ceremonial guard. Their weapons were all loaded and each one of them constantly checked their surroundings, looking for potential threats, including the ever-present problem of improvised explosives and booby traps. Their armour was painted in mottled grey urban camouflage and two of the marines wore heavily scarred and marked armour. It was a matter of pride to not cover up or repair damage, providing it didn't affect the integrity of the suit. The Admiral stopped for a moment and surveyed the scene around her.

"Colonel, I still can't believe this station fell to the Zealots in the first place. We had ships, marines and weapons here, it should have never happened!"

"You're right, Admiral, it shouldn't but the insurgents have managed to infiltrate our colonial forces from military bases through to command staff. Not only did they seize army compounds on the surface, they managed to take a battleship as well. They are better trained and motivated than any of us could have imagined."

"Perhaps, still, it shouldn't be possible to get this far."

Multiple warships as well as the large military garrison with its formidable surface-based weapon systems had heavily protected the station. The design was in such a way that it should be able to hold off an entire capital ship on its own. With support ships and escorts it should have been impregnable to any organised force. The fact that lightly armed civilians attacked the station, successfully overrunning it for a matter of weeks, still astounded her.

What was more incredible to her though was that since the battle, the crippled and almost totally destroyed station was now back in use. The last time she had seen it up close had been through the view screens on her ship as it was being torn apart by battle. The video displays had shown the fighting on the surface as the marines fought their way through the strong defences and heavy weapon emplacements. A number of marine landing craft had crashed and burned in that operation, one that had cost hundreds of lives on both sides.

"We've come across over a dozen infiltrators in the last week. Some must have stayed hidden after the place was abandoned, the rest must have got here as stowaways. It's cost us another nine men trying to clear them out."

"I'm sorry to hear that, Colonel. Since I've been away you've had a tough time of it, I know. The good news however is that we now have three task forces, one here, one at Kerberos and the main Fleet at Khimaira. Our numbers have been increasing as missing ships or those that went into hiding have managed to reach the assembly points. It won't be long now before I have the numbers and resources on my side to go on the offensive," she said confidently.

Colonel Blake nodded in satisfaction.

"That is good to hear, Admiral. Since we lost the General and the ceasefire was implemented morale has taken a dive. Knowing we are about to get back into the fight will fire us all up."

"Don't you worry, Colonel, there is plenty of fighting left to be done," she said with a wry smile.

They pushed on past the partially cleared debris. The station would probably never be quite the same. The battle damage and self-destruct system had caused so much devastation it would take years to bring it back to anywhere near the position it had once been. In fact, at any other time it might have been abandoned permanently, but with secession fever spreading through the Proxima Star System, and no contact with the rest of the Confederacy in Alpha Centauri, she needed to hold on to any facilities and forces that she could. The two Star Systems formed the bulk of the Confederacy but the vast distance between them created problems in both communication and travel. Even the fastest manned ships took hundreds of days to make the trip and compressed laser communications took two months to travel from one System to the next. Not that the time difference really mattered at the moment, Alpha Centauri appeared to be having its own problems and all transport and communication was currently blocked between them. Admiral Jarvis' last orders from Naval Command had been to protect the citizens of the colonies and to crush the insurgency that was spreading before it was too late.

The Naval Station itself was large and capable of offering medical aid, repair crews and substantial combat support anywhere in the vicinity of the planet Prime that the station orbited. There were also a number of much smaller stations known as the Transit Stations and the surviving platforms from the battle had proven invaluable in getting supplies and equipment unloaded prior to being moved to Kronus. Down below only one of the seven colonies, Avagana, remained loyal to the Confederacy. Although fighting had stopped it could only be a matter of time before the secession forces made a final push to claim this colony. It was an odd situation whereby the strongest naval base and defences were orbiting a planet that was fairly hostile to Confederate control. As long as Avagana stood it was imperative that the Fleet maintained a stranglehold on the transit routes. The ships guaranteed the safety of the colony by interdicting any hostile forces trying to resupply units that might attack Avagana. Also, from this position reinforcements could be dropped directly into battle. It was a dark time for the Confederacy, a place where the violently independent colonies had been bickering and arguing for decades and had now found a voice in the guise of the new socialist dogma of the Church of Echidna. Four of the eleven planets in the system had already seceded and these included the only two habitable worlds, Kerberos and Prime. The remaining loyal colonies consisted of small planetary platforms, research bases and industrial complexes based around the dead worlds and gas giants in the System. As she considered the current tactical position her attention was drawn to an approaching man. The young Captain, his fatigues dirty and well used, stopped in front of the Admiral and saluted smartly.

"Admiral."

She stood for a short time, inspecting the man and simultaneously examining the space around them. He must have suspected something was wrong as his eyes drifted off to the side to a pile of heavy metal machinery and equipment before snapping back to the Admiral.

"Good work, Captain, Colonel Blake informs me your work teams are making excellent progress on the station. I was hoping it would be ready for basic repair work yet you've managed to bring a number of weapon systems online as well as establish workable medical facilities. Outstanding!"

"Thank you, Admiral. We have a good team here and they are bringing more and more of the equipment up to operational capability every day. I expect to have the primary shipyard cleared for dry dock work within forty-eight hours."

Admiral Jarvis walked along what had been the beautiful plaza and scene of the violent clash between the Zealots and marines. The debris had already been cleared but the damage to the structure was still very obvious. She moved slowly, still finding the lower gravity difficult to get used to. She had been on similar stations before and found it took a few days to get back into the rhythm of movement. It was common knowledge that extra weight could make life much easier and she had already adopted some of the salvage teams' gear, especially the grav boots. It was a fancy name but there was nothing fancy about a pair of boots whose only special feature was an extra twenty kilograms of weight added to the innersole via the dense polymer inserts.

"Tell me about the weapons, I thought the large calibre mounts were destroyed in the battle?"

"They were. We've been recovering equipment from the crippled hulk of Victorious. The ship is a wreck but lots of the systems are salvageable, especially those on the starboard section, they were the least damaged."

Admiral Jarvis considered the battle for a moment. It had been the most terrifying and violent ordeal she had ever faced when they put the Battlecruiser Crusader up against the rebel Battleship Victorious. After a long and deadly duel the Crusader had emerged the winner though at a very heavy cost. Even now the warship was still undergoing repairs at Kerberos along with a number of other vessels that had been in action since the uprising.

"How about the CiC, how badly damaged was it?"

"Well, not good, Sir. The self-destruct system pretty much destroyed the entire tactical system, the communication relays and all the power systems. We've set up a temporary power core and are moving systems down from the Bunker Hill and Santa Cruz to establish an operation data centre. I estimate it will take at least a week before all the systems are tied in and capable of providing wide band networking throughout the Fleet."

"Still, that is a good start. So in approximately a week we can start using the base here as the Sector Headquarters. I will ensure you are sent extra crews and equipment to help in your work."

"Thank you, Admiral, I should get back to my duties."

Admiral Jarvis nodded and returned the salute from the young man who then turned away smartly and rushed back to the many jobs he obviously needed to work on. No sooner had he left he was accosted by a several workers, each of them looking to him for information on the work projects. As the men went about their business the Admiral pulled out her datapad and examined the latest reports on the Fleet. There were a number of messages awaiting her attention but it was the one marked urgent that caught her eye. The subject simply read 'prisoners' and it could mean only one thing. Tapping the message it expanded out into a full report by the intelligence staff on the CCS Wasp, the light carrier and flagship of the small fleet in orbit around Prime.

The first part of the report outlined three potential leads in the disappearance of General Rivers and his unit.

The first two leads indicated a number of criminal gangs who were working on dangerous underground mining operation on Kerberos. The third lead came directly from comparing the previous two with the data recently arrived from the Tamarisk. It wasn't much but it did seem to point to one man, a trader with links to the slave trade on Prometheus. According to the associated data the information recovered by Commander Anderson and his crew indicated that a consignment of slaves and high value prisoners were being sent to Prometheus. There was no exact location or even total number of slaves though. The data was already out of date but the more Admiral Jarvis thought about it the more she was convinced it was the strongest lead so far. What could be higher value than the senior General in the Proxima System, other than her, of course?

Sliding her finger over the message she spelled out a set of revised orders as well as a full copy of the intelligence data to be sent to the Tamarisk. Hopefully the information would prove useful in their attempts to locate the General. As she pressed the button to send the encrypted and classified message back to the ship she noticed movement at the far end of the plaza. Placing the datapad back into its pouch she made her way to the observation windows where a small number of workmen had already moved to. As she approached a few of the men spotted her and quickly moved back, one of them coughed to get the attention of the rest before she arrived. Upon reaching the toughened and recently replaced glass she looked out at the moving shape.

"It's the Resolution, Sir," said one of the workers.

"The Resolution? I thought she was a hulk."

Admiral Jarvis watched the massive grey ship move slowly away from its mooring and towards one of the cleared dock areas.

"I don't think she's functional," she said pointing out to the bow of the ship. "If you look carefully, Colonel, you can see the tugs pulling her away from the station. According to the damage report though it seems that with a repaired core and a new fire control system installed she might actually be usable."

"I don't understand, I thought she was already crippled beyond use in the battle for the station? When our marines took the station she was out of action already. If her guns had been active it would have been a suicide mission."

"True. It looks like the crew were able to sabotage the ship before it was overrun. They damaged the power corps and destroyed all of the fire control system making her dead in the water and impotent."

As they watched the vessel move away Admiral Jarvis rechecked the battle damage again on her datapad. By her calculations, if there were any chance of getting the heavy cruiser patched up it would help boost her meagre forces to something a little respectable. Though the numbers were not all in yet she had a confirmed list of six capital ships, three marine assault transport ships and up to eighteen frigates plus an unknown numbers of cutters, corvettes and destroyers. It was hardly a fleet worth of the Great War where dozens of capital ships gathered for apocalyptical battles. It might be enough though to conduct significant operations in this System. At present she was down on heavy warships with both the Crusader and Vengeance undergoing substantial repairs.

"I think I've seen enough. If you'll excuse me, Colonel, I need to return to the CiC. Please continue as you were, you are running an excellent operation and I have no doubt that both the station and the Fleet will be fully operational and ready to conduct combat operations in a matter of days."

The two officers saluted before turning to their previous duties. As the Admiral marched off the Colonel turned and watched just for a moment as she disappeared into one of the many corridors, closely escorted by her bodyguards. He turned back to the work crews and shouted out to a small group of men working on a power coupling.

"Chief, where are we on the Point Defence System?"

The short, slightly overweight man in the orange jacket of the deck chief lowered his tools and spoke a few words before getting up and walking towards the approaching officer.

"Sorry, Sir, what was that?"

"I need an update on the PDS?"

"We're hitting a few problems. The power lines to the core were fried in the attack and we have to reroute them through the old copper lines. The output is a lot lower but I reckon we can have about half the system up and providing basic defensive screening in about twenty hours."

"Good, good. Any chance of getting the full system up after that?"

"The full system? No way, we'll have to rebuild the entire power network for that. I'd need about fifty men and two months minimum to do that, Sir."

"What if I could get you two hundred men and all the power lines and hardware I can salvage from the carcass of the Victorious?" asked the Colonel with a slightly raised eye.

"Well, if you can pull that off I reckon we can get it done in about a quarter of the time. If you can scrounge the power lines from the ship we could even get some of the primary anti-ship railguns running again, Sir."

"Alright, consider it done. I'll see you again tomorrow and I'll bring you news on the hardware you need."

The Chief smiled before realising quite how much extra work he had just volunteered for. He opened his mouth to respond but the Colonel was well gone.

CHAPTER FIVE

Cases of cell mutation were first recorded on the manned missions to Mars back in the old Solar System. Direct exposure to radiation with little shielding resulted in abnormalities and many children were born with deficiencies and long-term problems. Screening of newborns was the only option until the development in the late 21stcentury of adequate radiation shielding equipment. Even then some of the more crude ships and bases lacked decent protection until the mid 22ndcentury. By this point, tens of thousands had been affected and the scourge of mutation became a known and terrifying problem.

Lessons on Mutation

Spartan stood in line along with what must have been about another hundred prisoners. They'd been granted just a few hours sleep before being forced to meet in the main hall of their wing in the compound. The internal structure was crude and certainly not a military or research laboratory site. Though there was much space, this part of the facility had been built by simply blasting through the hard rock on the planet to create living space. There was no heating, not that it was needed, as all the stonework was warm to the touch but not too hot that it burned. The side effect was that the overall temperature was hot and it made breathing and sleeping difficult. As he stood there Spartan could see the sweat dripping from the prisoners, each one of them losing substantial amounts of water.

In front of the group was a nasty looking man. He was short and squat, stripped to the waist and carrying a coiled whip on his side. Dotted throughout the area were a number of armed guards, some watching the group the rest just relaxing, obviously used to the day-to-day grind at the compound.

"My name is Vespis and this place is your new home, it is also your last home!" shouted the little man as he paced along the group.

"Some of you are here because you owe money, others because of your crimes and the rest for just being assholes! I don't care though because now you belong to me!" He then stopped in front of them.

"Remember what the Governor told each of you, the entire site is protected by automated sentry units as well as over a hundred armed guards. There are only two ways out of this compound. One is by visiting the surface. That is a one-way ticket by the way and the punishment for repeatedly breaking our rules or refusing orders. The second is a lottery for those who do as they are told. Each day a random selection of you will be given the only opportunity you will ever have to leave here alive. This is a trip to the re-education and social rehabilitation centre."

Spartan wasn't interested in the options right now, all he could think about were the numbers of guards in the facility. Over one hundred was a massive amount. A hundred guards must mean there were thousands of prisoners, maybe more. This was a much bigger operation than he had ever expected.

"If you obey the rules you will receive privileges." He raised both hands up and as if by magic it seemed, a loud buzz echoed through the chamber before settling to a low hum. At first it wasn't clear what was actually happening until a blast of cool air moved into the open space. It felt as if they were standing outdoors in a light breeze before it eased and started to reduce the overall temperature.

"The entire compound has its air scrubbed and cooled, that goes for this area too. Every section can be cut off and experience shows you will sweat out every last drop of water in hours. Any breaking of the rules will result in a six-hour penalty with the scrubbers switched off. Anybody breaks the rules twice and you pay a visit to the surface. That is the one-way trip!" he snarled and then waited for the information to sink in.

"Now, there are plenty more people coming from where you came from. You're cheap and we can afford to lose some of you working here, so don't fuck around!"

There was a stunned silence in the hall as the prisoners stood in a mixture of fear and relief at the switching on of the scrubbers and coolers. Cool air or not, it was obvious to them all that this was a one-way assignment and some were already showing signs of they would probably give up early.

"Each of you will be assigned a coloured band which you will wear at all times. The colour will indicate your group for work, rest and training. Failure to wear your band will constitute a breaking of the rules. Failure to comply with the orders of our officials or guards will constitute breaking of the rules."

He turned and continued walking, looking at the odd prisoner and then moving along. As he came closer Spartan did his best to avoid eye contact but it didn't work. The short man stopped directly in front of him and looked carefully at his face.

"You...you have military or combat training don't you? Which unit?"

Spartan was torn between telling the arrogant toad the truth revealing a secret that might be dangerous, or lying and being caught out. Both options could be as severe as each other. He decided to take the middle road and use an earlier truth, answering in a slow, monotone voice.

"I used to be a pit fighter."

"Fighter, huh? We have fighters at the pits here on Prometheus. Ever fight on the station circuit here?"

"Yes."

The little man stepped back with a smile on his face.

"Good, then you must be the first volunteer for the red group. Take this and stand over there!" He handed Spartan a red elasticated band. He slid it on and looked over to where he was supposed to stand.

"Don't make me tell you twice!"

Spartan didn't wait, he moved forward and towards the space a short distance from the rest of the prisoners.

"The red group is what I like to call the special group. It will get the toughest assignments but it will receive benefits and the chance to win your freedom. Anybody who works in the red group for one continuous week will be sent to our education programme. From there you will be," he coughed quietly to himself, "reintegrated into society."

Spartan was hardly an intellectual but he could see the man was lying. Whatever this re-education thing was it wouldn't be for any kind of freedom. The question was though, did he want to stay in the prison forever or did he want to try for the re-education and see if it would improve his chances of escape? As he stood there thinking, the man had stopped and was talking to more of the prisoners. It didn't take long before the red group had expanded to twelve men and two women. There was one thing they all had in common. They were the fittest and strongest. That one fact scared Spartan more than anything else he had seen or heard in the last hour. They hadn't selected General Rivers or Marcus as he could see they were still with the rest of the prisoners. Their lack of strength and injuries may have put the man off from selecting them, assuming there wasn't another reason.

"What the hell are they planning?" he muttered quietly to himself.

Two more men in suits arrived and started handing out more of the bands but this time they appeared to be passing them out indiscriminately. As this continued the short man moved to the red group and checked each of them before stopping in the middle.

"Come with me." He then turned about and walked away.

As he left two of the guards went alongside him and another four behind. A few of the red group started to move, then as if one they all walked away in a short, snaking column. They went towards the far side of the cavernous area to a locked bulkhead door about five metres wide. As they approached, the domed security units activated and scanned the group. The short man spoke quietly to the units that immediately turned around, their glowing red eyes watching the prisoners closely. As they were walking past the security system Spartan felt a horrible chill through his body when he noticed one of the red eyes turning to follow him. It was strange but he was convinced it adjusted and altered its focus as it watched him. Nothing happened though and just a short while later they were going uphill along a much more modern corridor. Unlike where they were sleeping, the walls were ribbed with metal and a series of low level lights guided them on their way. Continuing on, they were led up to a point where a bright dot of a light could be seen. As they continued moving Vespis, the man with the whip, called out to them.

"When you reach your destination, just remember one thing, anyone who tries to leave or refuses to co-operate will be returned to the general population. Do it again and you will be sent to the surface for a little sun bathing."

Spartan tried to work out what was ahead but the low light in the corridor, coupled with the bright light in the distance, made it impossible to make out any kind of detail other than that the light was becoming bigger.

"Where are we going?" asked one of the prisoners, a tall, strong looking man with a series of scars across his chest.

Spartan looked back, assuming he was talking to the man behind him but when his gaze returned he noticed the man looking at him. Spartan shrugged.

"Look, man, I'm not stupid. They took the strongest and put us together. From what the guy at the front said we aren't going to like it."

"You're probably right," answered Spartan laconically.

They were now only a short distance away and could see that the light was coming from a large open space that led out from the corridor. As they moved to within twenty metres Spartan spotted the first two guards, both in very heavy armour and equipped full modern rifles. They carried on and he was unsurprised to notice the markings on the armour, the same kind of snake symbol he had seen on the other armoured men. The doors were already open in front of them and in seconds they were all out of the corridor and in a large expanse of probably fifty metres radius. The perimeter and ceiling were masked in blackness, the only light coming from a wide skylight that lit up the centre of the place with a bright white light.

"Stop!" shouted their leader who then moved back to face them.

"This room is used as a test area for various subjects. We are looking for the strongest and those with the greatest survival instincts for a special project. It means better living conditions and movement to the re-education centre where you will eventually be placed back into society."

"Who put you in charge? Why are we here?" shouted a wide and powerful looking Asian man at the back of the group.

"It doesn't matter who we are. You are the prisoners and we are all that stands between life and death for you all. You may leave at any time, just ask for it and you will be taken out and released onto the planet's surface," he said as he leered at them.

"Bastard!" shouted one of the men though he kept down low enough to not be seen.

"You are all flawed, but you can take this as your opportunity to make amends. Remember...you can leave whenever you want." With an evil smile he turned to a box that had just risen out of the floor.

"Inside this box is a random selection of items. In ten minutes you will face a dangerous and deadly challenge. Those of you that survive will stay in the red group and return to your sleeping quarters at the end of the test."

There was a deafening silence as they stood in disbelief. Spartan looked about the group and then to their tormentor. "What if we chose to not participate in your test?"

Vespis simply stood and stared at them for almost half a minute before speaking.

"It is very, very simple. If you refuse to participate you will rejoin the rest of the prisoners and force a group punishment for breaking the rules."

"Screw this, I'm leaving!" shouted a scrawny looking man with long blond hair and thick, muscular arms.

"Two breaks of the rules and you will be sent to the surface where you will be in the fire of Prometheus!" He lifted his head and hand up high with an odd cackle in his voice.

"What the hell is this guy's problem?" muttered Spartan, a few of the others grumbled in agreement.

"The only other option available to you is to follow through with the test and to fail it. Failure is an option but one I think you might want to avoid!" he laughed and then started to move away.

"What's going on here? Hey, you!" shouted an oriental woman who pushed to the front and reached out. She tried to touch the man but two of the armoured guards stepped in to block her path. Spartan grabbed her and pulled her close until her head was pushed up to his chest.

"Don't do that," he whispered, "do you want to burn?"

The woman pushed away and wiped her brow as she stared at Spartan. Of all them in the open area he was the only one that looked unfazed by what was happening. The man and his guards left quickly, leaving them all stood in the bright light of the high ceiling mounted light burning down to the box in the middle of the room.

"What is this place?" asked the woman.

"Looks like a yard to me," answered one.

"No way, man, it's another prison area," said another.

"I know what this place is!" said Spartan with a firm tone in his voice.

As the rest of the group started to move about, Spartan stood his ground and looked down at the floor and the scratches and markings. He knelt down and rubbed his hand on the floor, feeling the deep cuts and imperfections.

As he concentrated on the floor the oriental woman approached him. Spartan sensed somebody moving and looked up to see her getting closer. Though her clothes were dirty and ragged he was surprised to see the poise and strength in her figure. He looked up at her pale face. Her ruffled hair ran down to just below the neck where it ended in rough curls. It must have been dyed as it contained streaks of blonde that were not her natural colour.

"Who are you?"

"Spartan. Why?"

She looked back at the rest of them, two were pulling open the box and scattering the items across the floor.

"You seem to be the only one who doesn't seem afraid."

"You're wrong there. Only a fool wouldn't be afraid in this place," He looked back to the floor. The young woman moved closer and bent down to examine the floor with him. She ran her hands along the cracks and pits in the stone, noticing the residual warmth coming up from the planet's molten rivers that boiled beneath the surface.

"What is it?"

"This place, it's an arena." He started to stand up, as he moved she followed until they both stood facing each other.

"Arena? Like a sports field?"

"No, like a pit fighting arena."

"What did you say?" shouted a tall, dark skinned man. Spartan ignored the man and turned back to the woman.

"Look, they are going to make us fight something and the only way we're staying alive is if we win. What's your name?"

"Misaki Satō."

Spartan nodded and then turned to the rest. Some of them had already taken items from the box and it was a bizarre collection of artefacts. There was a selection of hand tools, axes and metal fittings. One man stood with an axe resting on his shoulder as another two argued over a serrated knife.

"I used to be a pit fighter, I've seen this before. How many of you have combat training?"

Some ignored him but most turned to answer. It seemed they had a modicum of training, or at least that is what their raised hands told him. Misaki lifted her hand too.

"You have combat training?" asked Spartan with a raised eyebrow.

"Why? Can't a woman know how to fight?" she said with a wicked smile before scuttling over to the box to look for a weapon.

As she rummaged about she picked out what looked like a piston from the innards of an internal combustion engine. She grasped it by the small part to create an improvised mace. With a little more digging she started to tug at something in the base of the box. Before she was able to remove the object though a great rumble echoed throughout the chamber. At the same time a grinding sound like that of a heavy rock being dragged came from one side of the open area. Misaki fell back from the box, in her hands she grasped what looked like a metre long iron pipe. She steadied herself and called over to Spartan.

"Hey, Spartan...catch!"

She tossed the metal pipe and for just a second it looked like it might collide with his head. His reaction was fast enough and he easily caught it, swinging it around for a few test strikes before resting it on his shoulder.

"Yeah, I thought it might be more your style!" she laughed as she flashed a smile in his direction.

"I wouldn't get too excited. If I'm right we're about to get into something bad, really bad."

As if to emphasise his point the grinding stopped to be replaced by the pound of feet as something large and dark approached. Most of the fourteen of them were now carrying objects from the box. Two rushed back to the entrance they had arrived from as the rest stood in silence, each watching for whatever was about to appear before them.

"Stick together and stay in the light!" shouted Spartan as he moved into the centre.

Misaki moved ahead and joined him, standing just a metre away to his right.

"What is it?" she asked.

From the darkness the shape took form as the thing moved towards them. One of the men, a tall man about the same size and build of Spartan rushed forward with a bar in his hand. He disappeared into the shadows so that the approaching thing and the man merged into a moving shadow. There was just a single crunching sound and the man stumbled back into the light and fell back to the floor.

Misaki ran to him and rolled the man over. A trickle of blood ran down his face and a dark pool of blood started to form around him. She leaned down and listened for signs of breathing. She shook her head in shock as she looked back to Spartan.

"He's dead!" she shouted.

* * *

Kowalski sat at his display, idly moving data about and occasionally playing one of the video games he'd secretly brought to the vessel and installed on the system. It was hardly a modern game in fact by any standards it was ancient. The game was based on a security system whereby the player had to rewrite code on the fly to circumvent the computer which was doing the same. It was a test of speed, programming and mental dexterity. Though the language it used was obsolete it did keep his mind active and the basic algorithms were sound.

"Come on, come on!" he shouted as streams of data rushed down the screen.

The computer player had managed to breach his final

firewall and data was pouring from his servers. His fingers darted about on the touch based screens as he moved blocks of code into place and ran a series of subroutines that damaged the scrambled outgoing data as he attempted to repair the breach. A box popped up in the middle of the display and the game paused, the race against time now stopped until he was ready to resume.

"No way!" he muttered as he read the subject of the message before turning to the intercom.

"Commander, we've got a Fleet transmission, looks like they've found something."

There was a short pause before the groggy and tired voice of Commander Anderson returned on the speaker system.

"Understood, be there in sixty seconds. Get the rest of the crew in, we all need to see this."

"Affirmative." Kowalski hit a button to change the transmission to ship wide. "Kowalski here. We have a Fleet transmission regarding our mission. Please meet in the control centre immediately. This looks important, out."

As he replaced the handset he looked at the heading of the message and tried to imagine what they might have found. He was tempted to view the message but it required an access code that although he had, it would immediately let the Commander know he had read it first. He sat, staring into the screen as the Commander arrived.

"Kowalski, thought you'd have had it decoded and read

by now," he said smiling.

"Well, it is addressed for your eyes only, Sir."

The Commander leaned in to read the text of the message before entering in his hex based security code. It took a few seconds for each of the layers to be removed before it was displayed in all its detail. As well as a message from Admiral Jarvis it included several dossier documents with attached images and videos. Bishop and Teresa arrived almost at the same time and pulled themselves into position around the display.

"What have we got?" Bishop asked.

"Any news on Spartan?" added Teresa.

Commander Anderson looked at a few more of the documents before turning back to them.

"It is interesting. From the data we sent them they have matched it to other intel and come up with three possible leads. The main one though is to do with this man, Maximilian Hex. He's a smuggler and slaver known to work in these waters. The lead points to a shipment of slaves and high value prisoners being sent to Prometheus. There isn't an exact location but data from patrols in that area show increased numbers of ships around the planet."

Bishop looked at some of the information, specifically the dossier on Hex.

"I don't see why they are so sure this guy is the one we need to find. So he deals in slaves, so do hundreds of traders through the System."

"For a starter look at the numbers of ships recorded moving to Prometheus. There has been a forty per cent increase in the last three weeks. Most of these vessels are unflagged and not on our system."

"True, Sir, but couldn't they be refugees from the colonies that have seceded? There must be hundreds of thousands of displaced people?" asked Kowalski.

"There is one more piece of information from an informant on board a transport near Prometheus. He hasn't seen the prisoners but he did hear a rumour about one of the ships that arrived from Kerberos in the last week. He said a group of prisoners managed to fight their way out of their cells and killed a large number of security people."

"Bishop didn't look convinced but Anderson continued.

"Well, it's the only recorded time that anyone has managed to escape on board a slave or prison ship. There was one other thing...a number of those killed was in close quarter combat."

"Close quarter? That sounds like Spartan!" said Teresa with a growing smile.

"Give me the details, I'll run it through the local net and the Prometheus trading markets and see if I can come up with some leads," said Kowalski.

He leaned forward and started to move windows of data around the displays. At first he checked public markets and news stories, then law enforcements bulletins and coastguard and customs data. There was so much material whizzing about that the rest of them finally gave up trying to track his progress. Then he stopped, a single window with a blurred photograph and a few lines of text showing.

"There he is!"

"You crazy bastard!" laughed Bishop as he ruffled Kowalski's hair.

"Look, it says here that he has a public sale of licensed armour and tooling on the Prometheus Seven Trading Post for the next ten days."

"No way, it takes months to make that trip. You know, the storms. You have to plot a new navigation route every time you head for the place."

"Yeah, it's true. Bishop's right about the storms," said a miserable Teresa.

"Not true!"

They all looked at Kowalski who simply ignored them, he was far too absorbed in the details of Hex and his business dealings on Prometheus. It must have been fascinating because Commander had already called out his name three times before he responded.

"Uh, yeah?" he asked, looking a little confused.

"Prometheus. What isn't true?"

"Oh, right, well...the storms and the routes used by civilian and military traffic. You can bypass the lot and cut the trip to about four days."

Bishop looked at the Commander, who appeared less than convinced, and then back at Kowalski who sat there looking calm and collected.

"Bullshit!"

"It's true, Bishop. I submitted a paper on it over a year ago. The algorithm I developed will allow a nav system to plot a route through the storm with a ninety-two per cent safety margin. You need a decent system, one that can multitask multiple routes in real time along with updated storm tracking information from the naval buoys."

"You're serious?" asked Commander Anderson.

Kowalski looked at him for a few seconds before replying.

"I'm always serious, Sir, when it comes to tech. Trust me, my system works. The chance for loss is there, but it is the fastest and most direct route to Prometheus."

"Why haven't I heard about this?"

"First of all the risk is considered too high for manned vessels and the travel speed needs to be reduced according to the mass and rated engine power of the ship. Even a haulage or transport ship will have to drop speed to give a total journey time of about two weeks. Any faster and the computers won't be available to avoid the storm anomalies. Second, the first demonstration to the brass resulted in a simulated passenger liner being destroyed. I told them to use a smaller ship but they insisted. Something that big at the speed they used had only a fifty per cent chance of making it through."

"I believe you. Back when I was a captain out on the Rim I sent reports back that were ignored in favour of more reliable sources. It's the price we pay for being out of the loop. So as I understand it you're telling me a slaver could have made this trip in about two weeks if they had your algorithms?"

"Sure, no problem. How would they have got them though?"

"The computer data centre on Kerberos was hit during the riots and protests. I think we lost many guys when it was stormed. A lot of data was taken before it was cut off from the main data feed. It's possible they could have got it there," suggested Bishop.

"Maybe, or somebody could have just sold the software code. It would be worth a lot of money on the black market."

"Kowalski, are you sure the Tamarisk could do the trip in four days? I know she is bigger than most small transports but she's been refitted with a more powerful computer, engines and power plant."

"I've already done the calculations, Sir. We can be there in ninety three-hours if we leave right now."

Commander Anderson looked at the rest of his crew. There were only four of them now but they were becoming almost a family. Bishop an experienced Marine Corps veteran and Kowalski his best friend, one of the top techs in the Corps. Then Teresa, the demure but hot headed Hispanic fighter, who seemed to have limitless energy when it came to getting what she wanted. Anderson himself had been the XO of the Battlecruiser Crusader but this job was something special and needed his skills that he had learned taking on the organised crime syndicates out on the Rim. He just hoped that when this was all done and finished he could get back to being number two on the flagship.

"Good, confirm the course for Prometheus and get going at maximum speed. I'll contact the Admiral. I suggest you all check the files on our destination. It is not the place to arrive at unprepared."

"Sir!" came the almost instantaneous reply from his crew.

As the Commander moved away from the computer and along the corridor, Bishop turned to look at the other two. Kowalski looked completely unaffected by the turn of events and moved back to looking at the data, Teresa's face on the other hand was positively glowing.

"You look like you've hit the jackpot."

Teresa raised one eyebrow as she looked back at him.

"Well, this gets us one step closer to them doesn't it?"

"Let's hope so," he said and then turned back to Kowalski. "Can you get the schematics of the Prometheus Seven Trading Post? What kind of place is it?"

"No problemo, here it is."

On the display a rotating model of the large station appeared. It wasn't military, or at least it didn't have the look of any of the naval stations used throughout the System. As the model rotated it seemed the station was not far off the size of the station on Kronus.

"How big is that place?"

"It's big, I mean real big. It's based on the early Bernal sphere design, it's intended as a long-term home for permanent residents but according to the data here the station has been moved from accommodation to mainly trade and commerce. It used to be called the Prometheus Seven Colony. It is almost two thousand metres in diameter, giving it a circumference of over six kilometres. At this size the station should be able to house anything up to one and two hundred thousand people."

"Why isn't it used as a colony anymore?"

Teresa cut in, "Since it was built a number of stations have been built on the moons and there are scores of compounds on the surface that use the planet's heat to drive thermal generators. Apparently much of the population moved during the last few decades to the surface and the new cities being built there are well shielded. Still, give me a lush green world with air and an actual breathable atmosphere."

"Screw that, Teresa," muttered Bishop, "all the images I've seen of Prometheus make it look like hell."

"It is. You get used to it though. When I worked there

I spent most of my time on the stations but I did do a bit of manual labour underground. Trust me, you don't want to work there. Doesn't matter how much they pay you, it isn't worth it!"

She looked back at the display and smiled. "Somewhere out there are Spartan, Marcus and the General. And you know what? We're going to find them!"

* * *

"Help me!" cried Misaki as she tried to massage the expired man on the ground. It was pointless, his heart had stopped, he wasn't breathing and the pool of blood was increasing. It looked like there was little chance anything could be done. Even so Misaki refused to back down and continued the heart massage in the grim hope something might change.

"Come on, let's out of here!" shouted one of the men as he banged on the now closed door.

The rest of them stood still, all waiting for the thing to emerge from the shadows. Spartan moved in front of Misaki and the fallen man and held the metal pipe on his right shoulder like a baseball bat.

"Misaki, he's dead, come on!"

Misaki ignored him though her frustration was obvious. She carried on pounding at the man's chest and shouting out.

Spartan looked in the direction of the shape that moved out into the light. Of all the people in the open space only Spartan seemed unperturbed by the great hulk. It was a Biomech, one of the creatures that Spartan had come across several times now. After these encounters he was still in awe of the mass and power of these things. This one looked more like the ones he had seen in the urban combat operations on Prime. It was armoured up with improvised metal plates and carried what looked like a heavy iron maul in each hand. With a roar the Biomech moved directly into the light and planted its feet, glancing around as the people scattered through the open space.

"Misaki!" called out Spartan as he stood his ground.

The young woman picked herself up and moved up to him, her own improvised mace out and ready.

"What is it?" she asked, a trembling tone in her voice.

"It's one of those Biomech shock troopers the Zealots have been using, keep away from it!"

Pushing in front he swung his metal pipe, drawing the attention of the creature. Three of the other people moved towards Spartan, either for safety or recognising that he seemed to know what he was doing. The creature stood still, as though it was waiting for an order. As the rest waited a shrill whine blasted from hidden speakers.

"Welcome to our little training arena. In front of you is one of our pets. He is the smallest and youngest. Today's test is to survive until the bell hits ten chimes. There are no rules, just survive until the time runs out!"

The creature roared and rushed ahead directly towards Spartan. He stood still and waited, his weapon in position and ready for the fight.

"Let's do this!" Spartan shouted and to their surprise he ran forward to meet it head on.

"Spartan!" Misaki screamed as she watched him rush directly into the path of the monster. It was like a tale from Ancient history with a mythical hero tackling a Minotaur or other ferocious beast.

As Spartan reached striking distance it swung its right arm and brought the mace on a collision course with Spartan's head. The bell struck one and at the same time the mace whistled towards his face. With incredible speed and timing he ducked down at the last minute and leaned out to strike the passing creature in the back of the knee. It might have been bigger and stronger than any of them there but its knees were still vulnerable to an attack. As his metal bar struck the thing lots its balance and slid onto its back, flailing about in anger. Spartan stood up and turned around to look directly into its eyes. He stepped forward but it was already up off the ground and snarling. A few of the prisoners rushed from the side to try and take advantage of the moment to strike. The bell struck again.

"No! Stay back!" shouted Spartan. They either didn't hear or didn't care.

The first man stabbed hard with a small knife only to

find it got stuck in the creature's thick hide. It swung its left arm and struck the man in the temple with its mace. The crunch of bone made a terrible sound and the man was dead before his lifeless corpse hit the ground. The others waved their weapons and made ineffectual strikes but with the death of their comrade they lost the will to close the distance.

Spartan pushed forward and swung his bar in an arc just a short distance from its face. The attack missed but did force a response. Instinctively the creature tried to parry the strike but hit nothing but air. Its inexperience showed as it twisted around and exposed its right flank. Spartan wasted no time in slamming the heavy metal hard into its ribs and breaking at least two of them. One of the women jumped forward and managed to hit the creature on the head but hit the armoured skullcap causing nothing but a loud sound. The bell continued to ring though none of them were paying attention, just concentrating on staying alive. It swung at the woman but Misaki managed to jump in striking the weapon aside with her own mace and then drag the woman to safety.

"You!" shouted Spartan as he pointed his weapon at the creature. It roared at him though there were no intelligible words, just animalistic noises.

It swung the maces, clearing the rest of the prisoners away until a small, loose line of them stood with Spartan on the right of the group. As it moved forward one step at a time they move in around Spartan, finally understanding that their best chance lay with him. They prepared for another attack when the bell rang out for the tenth and final time. In synchronisation with the sound a series of lights came on around the arena.

The creature stopped its attack and lowered its weapons, whether it was a signal from the lights and sounds or it was simply used to the procedure was unclear. All they did know was that for now the fight was over. The whistle from the speakers came back, followed by the man's voice. As he spoke the beast turned away and returned to the large doorway from where it had entered the arena. As it approached the door slid open revealing four heavily armed guards with their weapons pointed at the prisoners.

"Congratulations. Some of you have passed your first test," came the voice from the speakers.

The entry door opened with a dull grinding sound and two of the prisoners who were still lurking nearby jumped through and into the arms of the waiting guards who pushed them back inside.

"Follow the guards backs to your quarters, you will face a new and much tougher test tomorrow."

The sound cut off and the guards beckoned for them to follow as several men in lab coats approached the two bodies and started to lift them onto stretchers.

"What the hell is this place?" Misaki asked.

Spartan looked at the guards and then back to her.

"I don't know, one thing I do know," he said before leaning in closer to her, "I'm not waiting around to find out."

CHAPTER SIX

It is one of the ironies of the new colonies in Alpha Centauri that some of the oldest nationalities from Earth would come to find new homes in Space at the expense of the old world on Earth. Whereas in the past Italians, Germans and British citizens had flocked to the New World of the Americas a new wave of colonists travelled to such places as Carthago and Terra Nova to establish new communities that worked hard to stay true to their old routes.

British communities on Terra Nova still fly the flag on traditional public holidays and the National Flags are still worn by some on their military uniforms, as is the right of all citizens of the Confederacy. Italian-Novans constituted some of the earliest Confederate Army units.

The Old World meets the Newer World

"Spartan, is that your real name?" Misaki asked.

The two were sat on the wooden benches running along the side of their quarters, along with the survivors of the first confrontation with the Biomechs. The quarters for the red group was cramped but seemed at least a few metres bigger than what the rest had to manage with.

"Yeah, it's my name."

"That's it? You must have another name?"

Spartan said nothing, either he was too tired to speak or not prepared to say anymore. Misaki waited for a little longer before speaking again. They had all had a thorough medical examination before being given their uninspiring overalls. The colour was a kind of faded orange and at some time they must have belonged to a company as the logos had all been ripped off, leaving small patches and holes in various places.

"What do you think is going on here?"

This question seemed to get Spartan's interest, even making him sit up and look at her briefly before speaking.

"A few things are pretty clear to me. First, this place is illegal. The weapons, armour and layout would have serious problems with Confederate control. Second, slave labour being used in pit fights is dodgy, very dodgy."

"How so?"

"Trust me, it is. The last bit though is those Biomechs. They are related to the Zealots and their masters in the Church of Echidna. Why are they here and why were some being transported to this place on our ship?"

"The Church of Echidna, aren't they the people who started the secession in the first place? I thought they were offering a peaceful, safer alternative to that of corporate control through the Confederacy?"

"You think so, Misaki? I've seen their peaceful ways, now you've seen them too!" he replied with a slightly raised tone that he immediately regretted.

From the far wall a pair of armed guards approached. They were again dressed in the dark body armour he'd seen when they arrived, each carried a shotgun and side arm. They were much more heavily equipped than any prison guards he had heard of. They moved up to the metal bars of their sleeping area and looked inside.

"What's going on in there?"

The guard was met with total silence.

"Yeah, that's what I'm talking about. Remember the rules, break them and you pay the price."

The second guard started to laugh, evidently enjoying the reminder of the power and control he had over the prisoners. He lingered a little too close though and Spartan was able to get a good look at his equipment and clothing. They waited a few more seconds before walking off to harass another group of prisoners.

"What were you looking for?"

Spartan lifted up his hand, waiting to make sure the guards were well out of sight and hearing before looking back at her. He indicated her to move closer. She crept forward, doing her best to make as little sound as possible and stopped close to his face.

"When we were being transported here I noticed the guards wore a snake symbol on their uniforms. Those guards had the same patch on their uniforms. I think it might be a department of one of the churches. Don't snakes have something to do with one of the religions?"

"Well, I do know that Echidna was half woman half snake and supposedly responsible for creating all monsters in the ancient world. Maybe that has something to do with it?"

Spartan scratched his chin as he considered the information.

"If these guards are part of a militant department or corporation they could easily be linked to the Church. They've been dealing behind the scenes for a long time I've been told and I would bet good money they supply the insurgents with money, weapons and intel."

"That makes sense, Spartan, the insurgents do have a lot in common with the Echidna missionaries. The next question though is what the hell are they doing here on Prometheus and even more important, why are we here? I've heard that there used to be all kinds of state funded research, especially biological and chemical science on this planet. Maybe the Biomechs are being brought here to be experimented on. They could be trying to improve or train them to be better fighters."

"Maybe. I've seen them in action though and they can fight perfectly well, they certainly don't need any more training to be effective. There's also the issue of all of us here. So yes, what the hell are we doing here?"

Misaki considered this for a moment.

"Good point. Prisoners are either being held here for political reasons or as a resource. From the way they treat us I'd say we're a resource."

"I agree."

Spartan heard something and lowered his head to avoid attracting attention. Of the small group remaining from the battle in the arena all were asleep or resting, each waiting for whatever hardship would be meted out next. One man lay on the floor, he had been groaning for the last hour from the heavy impacts he had sustained during the fight with the Biomech. Misaki was convinced it was broken ribs but neither the guards nor the other prisoners had much in the way of medical training. One of the guards re-appeared but this time he moved on past the bars and ignored them, he appeared content to just let them see him. As he moved off Misaki moved her face closer to Spartan's ear and whispered quietly.

"You said you've been on Prometheus before. How long ago was that?"

She leaned back to give him space but Spartan simply shrugged and ignored the question. Misaki raised an eyebrow in frustration but he refused to back down so she tried a different tack.

"Is that where you joined the Marine Corps? What happened then, did they ship you off right away?"

Spartan shuffled uncomfortably on the hard wooden surface.

"No, they posted me on a rookie transport and training programme through the sector. They told me it was a long trip from Prometheus to Prime, they say it's because of the storms, I don't think so though. I know ships have done it in a few months."

"So why did they take so long then?"

"I think it's more likely they were taking it slow to get green units like mine trained up for the meat grinder at the Bone Mill. I've heard since that the recruiting ships normally took newbies directly to Prime for training in a few months, they must have slowed down to get us trained before we hit the planet. If that's true they already knew we had people that couldn't be trusted on the surface."

"Sounds sensible to me, no point landing rookies directly into a warzone. Did you realise what was happening during your training?"

"No, we were all way, way too busy. I think we picked up extra recruits and equipment at stations on the way but they never told us where we were or where we were going. After a week's worth of training you don't really care which piece of black space you're travelling through, believe me!"

His mind drifted off to Teresa and their time on the Santa Maria. It was weird but those weeks of physical and mental endurance were some of the highlights of the last year for him. After years of moving from place to place he had bizarrely found a home amongst the rough but unpredictable world of the Marine Corps.

"How about you Misaki? What happened and why are you here?"

"Good question. I was on a colonial tour with my dance company when we were raided."

"Raided? Why?"

"There were some protests on Kerberos that our routines were, well let's say a little risqué!" she said with a sly grin.

"Strip dancing?"

"No...nothing like that. Our group is more like the old burlesque troupes you can sometimes see on Terra Nova."

"Never been to Nova, it's a long, expensive trip to the old worlds." He looked down at the floor in thought. "Wait, you said you were raided? By the police?"

"Well, we thought it was police at first which is weird because we were all licensed up to run shows on any colony we were invited to. The men wore no insignia but they were in normal riot police clothing. They said we had breached the peace and took us all away. Next thing I knew I was on the ship, in chains and drowsy."

"That doesn't sound like the police to me and these people definitely have links to the Zealots and their sympathisers."

They sat in silence for a few more minutes, each looking out through the bars and watching the lines of prisoners moving off for their allotted tasks and work projects. It seemed that they were able to avoid this extra work but only at the price of risking their lives by participating in the various tests the Governor had set. As Spartan sat there thinking he noticed Misaki watching him. Her face was tight and the stress obvious. He wanted to say something but couldn't think of anything particularly reassuring. She had been dragged from her work in almost the same manner as he was, all this just for performing some kind of dance. He thought about the dance she had talked about before realising he had no idea what she was talking about.

"Burlesque?"

Misaki looked at him intently, a little surprised at the question. "Yes?"

"I've never heard of it. What is it? Some kind of ethnic dance?"

"Not really. It is part dance and part act with an emphasis on style and sexiness. It can include striptease, garish costumes, bawdy humour, that kind of thing."

""Oh...I see." Though his response suggested the exact opposite.

As they sat in an uncomfortable silence a pair of the guards approached. Spartan looked at Misaki and then at the floor, giving her a visual cue to look down and avoid eye contact with their tormentors. The footsteps stopped, they were waiting outside the door. With a grinding sound the door slid open. Spartan turned to see the men pointing their weapons directly at his chest.

"Spartan?" the first asked.

"Maybe."

"Come with us, the Governor wants a word," the second ordered as he gestured with his shotgun for him to stand.

Spartan looked around the room, most of the prisoners were watching though none said a word for fear of reprisal from the guards. Spartan moved but before he could stand up the first guard took a step back.

"Take it slow...that's it, nice and easy." The guard appeared far more nervous than Spartan would have expected.

As he stood up a third, unseen man approached and attached a metal rod to Spartan's manacles. As before they could hold him off at a distance so he couldn't grab or kick at them. As soon as he was past the frame of the door it was quickly shut to stop anybody else following them. The first guard moved in front of Spartan. He came close but not too close.

"Play your cards right and this could be your ticket out...

soldier boy." He slammed his shotgun butt into Spartan's stomach.

Spartan dropped back and spluttered as the impact drove hard into his torso. It wasn't enough to drop him though and he quickly straightened up, his height and mass easily dwarfing the guard.

"Okay, tough guy, come."

With a push Spartan found himself moving behind the guard and followed by at least two more of them. Though he was desperate to escape there was nothing he could do when locked up and surrounded like this. As they moved away he looked around at the people coming back from their other duties. Most were filthy. They looked as if they had done hard physical work, possibly mining or construction. Based on the filth he thought the former was more likely. The guards continued nudging Spartan towards a cylindrical metal doorway at the side of the open space. It had no obvious markings or features and could easily have been some form of blast shield. The guard in front spoke into his helmet-mounted intercom unit. The words were too quiet for Spartan to make out but they must have been to give clearance to open the door. With a mechanical whirr the door slid around to the right to expose a small cylindrical room. The guards behind pushed him inside and followed closely. Once the four were all inside the door shut and low level white lighting illuminating the room. The floor shook and Spartan felt slightly lighter as the room went down at high speed.

"Where are we going?"

The guards ignored him, simply standing still and waiting. Somewhere in the walls a speaker system sent a series of codes and beeps but it meant nothing to him. He felt his legs becoming heavier again and then with a gentle bump they stopped. The door slid open to reveal a short corridor that led to a closed door. With a click the metal bar detached from his manacles and the guards stepped back inside the room. Concern for the unknown sent a shiver down his spine as he stepped out into the featureless corridor.

"Head to the door," ordered the guard and then the door slid shut leaving Spartan alone in the corridor.

It was weird, very weird. He had gone from being taken and guarded by heavily armed men, to now being totally alone with no sign of the enemy. He felt even more a prisoner than when he was manacled, at least then he knew where he was and had a certain expectation of what to expect. The door behind was of massively thick metal and sealed. The walls were smooth and hard and the only object that broke up the shape was the door at the end of the hallway. As he stood there he wondered if there was anything he could do other than approach the door. He touched the door behind him. It felt cool, much cooler than anything else he had been near since his arrival. The surface was ultra smooth, almost polished in appearance.

Pushing against it was no different to pushing against a stone wall, it refused to move even a millimetre. His gut told him to do something, anything other than what he had been told to do. It was pointless though, he had two choices, either wait or move ahead.

"Screw this!" he muttered and marched off for the door.

It might have led to something worse but the waiting was just as bad and if it was terrible he wanted it over with as quickly as possible. After his experiences in the ring and in combat he understood the unreasoning fear that gripped a man as he awaited his fate. With a final look behind he walked faster, ever watchful for anything, a marking, an object or handle that might give him cause for hope. He ran his hand along the wall, feeling for something. As he reached the door he found nothing, not even a scratch. Pushing his hand forward the door slid to the side to reveal a brightly lit room. The door was almost silent, more a hiss than a mechanical rhythm.

"Come in," came a firm voice from inside the room.

Spartan stepped forward, squinting at the light as he entered. With a whistle sound the door slid shut behind him. In front was a large metal desk and around the room what looked like cylindrical windows. Outside was the stillness and tranquillity of water. For a moment Spartan thought they were under an ocean but he quickly remembered they were on an inhospitable planet of fire and lava. Hardly the view you would want from your windows and definitely not a cool ocean. He thought to himself, was there even any water on the planet, before remembering where he was.

"I see you're admiring the view?" said the man sat at the desk.

Spartan said nothing, he'd already worked out they were deep underground and this room contained fake windows, much like the artificial windows on board the Confederate Navy vessels. By projecting an image onto the wall or a pre-allocated space the illusion of any location could be created.

"Nice view," replied Spartan in a calm a tone as he could muster.

"Quite," he replied, then took a gulp of water from a glass on the desk.

"You are probably wondering why I have asked for you to be brought to me?"

"You're Governor Richards?"

"Indeed. I see your memory is intact...good. Now, I have been reading your dossier and I see there are some, shall we say, slightly colourful episodes in your life over the last ten years?"

"I guess."

"You guess? I don't think so. A man with your background and training is wasted in the service of Marine Corps. Do they even know about your history before that unfortunate pit fight incident?"

"Incident? I was forced to fight to pay my debts, I had no choice!" Spartan was getting angry.

"I'm not really interested in that, I would rather hear your side of the story about the years before you joined the military. My contacts inform me that several members of your family were killed by colonial security forces, the forces who now serve the same master as yourself. Don't you find that a little ironic?"

Spartan fidgeted, he was uncomfortable as he listened to the man's questions. There didn't appear to be any guards and the room was bare apart from the two chairs, the desk and the windows. He thought of rushing ahead and grabbing the Governor but it couldn't be that easy, not a chance.

"You don't know about my family."

"Oh the contrary, I know all about your family. You will find our records are far more detailed than those of the so called Confederacy."

He moved his hand across the desk and brought up a series of virtual documents and photographs that he moved over to Spartan's side. He glanced at them but took no interest as the past meant little to him. He had always lived in the here and now and talking to this man was the price he had to pay while he worked out his escape plan.

"Did you know your parents were pilgrims? They were involved in the founding of some of the Church's most influential buildings. You don't remember them do you?"

"Remember what? It says on my records what happened to me and there is nothing about pilgrims or any other crap. Come on, your reports are shit. You don't even have my father's name!"

The man looked a little angry at his outburst and even a little disappointed.

"Your records state your parents died in a car crash when you were an infant. They found you near a burnt wreck and took you to hospital. Ten years later and you were still moving from children's homes. The interesting thing though is that we both know that isn't how it happened, don't we?"

Spartan had blocked out most of his childhood and he could feel the old memories starting to surface. With effort he forced them back down and looked at the Governor.

"I don't care about the past. I'm only interested in what happens next."

"The second part I don't doubt. Well, you're in luck, Spartan. As you may have noticed, unlike the Confederacy, our organisation is moving up in the world. This facility is one of many and it is going to provide a future for every soul in this System."

Spartan looked at him suspiciously. The mention of forces hostile to those he served felt alien to him, though he couldn't deny that the Confederacy had taken serious blows in the last months as the insurgency grew.

"You have probably already worked out that this isn't a Confederate facility, it isn't even an official Promethean outpost. This entire centre is owned outright by the Drakaina Research Corporation and the great work we are doing here will help change this entire System for the better." He pressed a few buttons at the end of the desk.

Spartan looked around the room and then back to where a number of three-dimensional diagrams appeared showing the layout of the complex. As he watched he was shocked to see how far underground the compound went. If this was true the site was easily twenty times bigger than he had thought, large enough to hide an entire colony if required to. The display altered slightly and followed several shafts moving out from the site.

"As you can see here, we are expanding into the bedrock where we will establish additional laboratories and factories. You might think we are treating you poorly, Spartan, but trust me, this is all for the greater good."

Spartan stared at him, his expression obvious. "Bullshit!"

"Quite," replied the Governor before continuing, "the Confederacy has never been strong. Each colony is independent, too independent while the political and military wings of the state have trouble maintaining order. It is inevitable that the structure will collapse, the only question is how many will die in the conflagration that will burn through every colony."

"How many will die? The insurgency is responsible

for the deaths of thousands already!" replied an angry Spartan.

"Some must die if the colonies are to be reborn into a single safe, powerful and secure empire for its citizens."

"And your solution for this is to stir up trouble so the colonies tear themselves apart?"

"We need to start from the beginning. A new slate if you will, and there is no point in trying to fight the Confederacy, even weakened it will fight for decades. With the help of people like you we can simply make the Confederacy impotent, remove them from the equation and replace them with a new, solid foundation as part of a new union of colonies."

Spartan shook his head. Though some of the ideas seemed reasonable he knew deep down that this man must be tied in with the insurgents and if that were true then their religious and social doctrine wouldn't be far behind. He'd already seen what religious fanaticism was capable of and he wanted nothing to do with it.

"Why are you telling me this?"

"It is my job to provide a large part of the resources needed by our people to rebuild this star system. As we sit here thousands of undesirables work to expand this complex, right under the noses of your Confederation lackeys. We are always looking for new recruits to lead combat forces and to represent the public face of the organisation."

For a moment Spartan was tempted to get physical and hit or strike, anything other than listen to the drone from this man. He really wasn't interested in politics but it was obvious something big was planned and he was being offered a chance to take part in it.

"Why would I want to join you?"

"A fair point. First of all, your training and skills have been brought to our attention. You have fought in multiple engagements where you have overcome overwhelming odds. We have many resources but we are always looking out for those with more specialist skills and the experience to do what needs to be done. If you join us you will become part of the solution, not the problem. The rewards will be great and in time you can expect to see your status improve immeasurably."

The Governor was obviously finished and placed both hands on the desk, indicating he wanted a response from Spartan.

"You aren't giving me the whole story here. Who exactly is 'us'? Your corporation doesn't operate on its own, what are your relations with the Church or the Zealots?"

"Relationship? Come now, surely you must have realised by now that there are no factions or interested parties involved. These are just names, the public faces for our movement. Join us and help change the Confederacy into what it should be."

Spartan had to force himself not to slam his fist onto

the desk. He was trying to think ahead but it didn't seem to be helping. He could of course say yes and try and work out a way to escape by working within the system or he could go back to the cell with the rest of the prisoners and await his fate. From what he had seen, if they were being put up against Biomechs every day then their days were numbered.

"Okay, I'm interested. I don't really care for the Confederacy one way or the other. It's just an employer for me and not one I would have chosen given the choice."

"Of course. I notice you were given the option of jail or service. If you are considering joining our enterprise we will need a demonstration of your loyalty, the same as for anybody else joining us. We expect and demand total loyalty and subservience to our authority for everyone. That goes from the lowliest of cleaners up through to our generals."

"Generals?" said Spartan involuntarily.

"Why of course. You think what you have seen so far represents all of our resources? We haven't even begun to unleash our forces. For now they are waiting, though people such as yourself could help shorten the length of any campaigns and ultimately save lives."

Spartan couldn't do it. His mind kept telling him to say yes, get out of the cell and try and work from the inside. The problem was that there were parts of the offer that appealed to him. The structure, the power and the resources to do something significant were a massive temptation. If he pushed he might even become a major commander who could mould and shape things in a way that might actually benefit people. The trouble was his gut told him he was lying to himself. He knew deep down that they would kill or enslave anybody opposed to their will. The relatively light hand of the Confederacy would be replaced by a totalitarian regime with strict laws, rules and religious decrees. As he considered the options the Governor sighed.

"I see you are unsure as to what you should do. I will take your lack of an immediate 'no' to be a 'maybe'. You can return to your cell, I suggest you give this a good think over. Just don't wait too long. Nobody has survived in the red group for more than two weeks and I think you'll find some of your friends will be joining you," he said with a dismissive smile.

The door slid open and in walked two of the guards, they looked like the ones that had brought him there but with the armour there was no way to be sure. He had just a few seconds before he was out of the room and in that brief moment he had just one question to ask.

"If I accept, can I bring others with me?"

"That is something we can discuss...if you decide we are your future. Just remember, you don't have long."

A hand on his shoulder pulled him to the door and before he could reply he was back in the corridor and making his way along the smooth surface to the sliding door. A light click behind them indicated the door to the room was now shut. Once they were three quarters the way to the door it hissed open to reveal another two guards who were standing alongside another prisoner. It wasn't anybody he recognised, she was a petite woman in her mid thirties with fiery red hair that was now matted and messy. As she moved towards Spartan in the corridor she turned and looked at him.

"What do they want? Three of my friends just died in the mines. What is happening?" she cried her voice becoming hysterical.

Spartan didn't know what to say and before he could speak they were pushed past each other and he was back inside the elevator. As the door shut behind him one of the guards leaned in towards his ear.

"Everybody joins in the end you know. It's just a matter of time. Leave it too long and you'll die in the mines or the arena. Your choice," he said before straightening up.

Spartan looked up at the dark visor, the face only partially visible under the glass.

"You?"

The guard said nothing and it looked like he was going to ignore Spartan. The elevator moved gently and they made their way back to their starting position. No light or markers indicated where they were and that told Spartan that the elevators were either controlled via the suits or they were being monitored from another location. He looked around at the featureless area until he spotted a slightly different coloured tile on the wall. He moved his head to one side and noticed it had a glossier surface than the rest. It must have been a camera mount or mirrored glass as it was the only feature there. The elevator started to slow down, now just a few seconds from the destination.

"I used to be in one of the gangs back on Kerb. You know, we shifted electronics, weapons and shit. Next thing I know, we get busted by some kind of team and sent to a camp. They told me I could join or work in their factory ships."

Spartan said nothing, surprised the man had spoken. The door hissed open to reveal the vast open space surrounded by the room-sized cells for each of the work gangs and groups. The first guard moved out and indicated for him to follow. As he moved the second guard leaned in and spoke quietly.

"This place is bullshit. They are making weapons for some kind of invasion. Get out!" he said in a whisper so that the other guard didn't hear.

Spartan was dumbfounded and his look could have easily given the guard away for the fact that he then struck Spartan in the shoulder.

"I said get to your cell, animal!"

Spartan staggered a few feet. He was angry but more at himself than the pain in his shoulder. On one hand he was being offered the chance to join the enemy and on the other he was being warned away. The only honourable thing was to stay and die, hardly a choice. They moved on further until they reached the bars and doorway to the red quarter where the rest of his group were. As the door opened he noticed some were eating food, others were trying to sleep.

As Spartan stepped inside he realised his manacles were fitted but unlocked. He turned back around but the two guards looked the same and were staring directly at him.

"Remember what I said!" said the guard to the right and then they were gone.

As quickly as they had arrived Spartan found he was alone with the rest of the prisoners who were waiting and looking as though they wanted to hear what had happened. Misaki rushed over to him and lifted her manacled hands up so should could lifted them over his head.

"I thought they'd taken you away!" she cried, grabbing on to him hard.

Spartan was taken aback by her actions but quickly relaxed. After a few moments she loosened her grip though her arms were still around him and holding him in tightly. He was surprised at her actions as they barely knew each other and had only spoken for a matter of minutes. He put it down to the stress and anxiety of the situation.

"What did they want?"

Spartan lifted her hands, freeing himself and then

slumped down to the wooden bench along the side. He hadn't been away long but returning to this filthy part of the compound reminded him of how low they could all fall. The smell was disgusting and the toilets were at the far end and exposed to all. Spartan shook his head, arguing with himself.

"Spartan! Tell me!"

"They want us to join them, to help remove the Confederacy with their new system."

"That's it? Is that so bad?"

"I don't know, Masaki. So far I haven't seen much to be positive about. Anything would be better than this place though."

Misaki looked at the rest of the prisoners and then back to him.

"When you were away a man arrived and told two of the men they had been selected for the re-education programme. They say a few people each week will be selected from the red group."

"Why this group?"

"Can't you see? Everybody here is the fittest and the strongest. Maybe they're testing us with the fights and challenges to weed out the best for whatever they are planning. Some kind of elite organisation maybe?"

Spartan considered her comments and although he doubted there was any kind of fancy organisation waiting for them he did agree with the system of selection. By taking the strongest survivors they would be receiving a steady stream of strong, fit, intelligent and healthy people. Maybe they were training them as Zealot troopers or perhaps something more insidious like eugenics or reproduction.

"If you go, will you take me?"

He didn't hear her, he suddenly felt very tired. Some of the lights started to cut out until the entire area was lit by just a small number of dull yellow lights. As the light faded so the electronic red lights of the night vision systems started to warm up. It might look dark but Spartan was certainly under no illusions he could be seen and probably heard at any time.

As he looked around open area he noticed a dark shape moving closer. He almost lifted his arms to strike when he heard Misaki speak again, this time she was almost touching his face. She must have moved around and directly blocked his line of sight.

"Spartan..." she whispered.

He felt her cool skin against him and then her face touched his. He tried to adjust his position as their lips met, both falling from the wooden benches to the hard and uncomfortable floor. Spartan flat on his back and Misaki draped across him. He tried to get back up but she held him down.

"Are you going to join them?" she said quietly.

Spartan lay there, saying nothing, just breathing quietly.

Not that he didn't like Misaki where she was, it was just the last time anything like this had been back on the Santa Cruz with Teresa. As he lay there thinking of her and what she must be doing right now he completely forgot about the half-naked Misaki still straddled across him. With a sigh of discontent she lifted herself up and back into the darkness, leaving Spartan to his thoughts.

CHAPTER SEVEN

Mechanical slave labour had been experimented with several times in the history of the Colonies. The most significant flirtations with the technology took place prior to the Great War and had led to three bloody riots and strikes by workers. The Confederacy after all was designed for its citizens and in the end a simple ban on machines that took the work of citizens was put in place. Even so, machines that could do jobs that humans could not were never outlawed and they were frequently used by the military. One reminder of this decision is some of the machine smashing festivals held by some families still on Kerberos.

History of Slave Labour

Commander Anderson stood against the wall, holding onto the rails as he looked at his prisoner. The man was locked in the brig, the smallest room in the entire ship and protected by ten centimetres of thickened metal all around. The man was still, looking back at the crew of the Tamarisk with the same level of interest that they held of him. Contrary to what he might think the Commander was no animal and he was almost certainly waiting for something violent and terrible to happen to him. Commander Anderson had spent a long time on the Rim and had experienced all kinds of crime and brutality but that had never changed his mind on physical torture, it had always been abhorrent to him. That didn't mean he couldn't use more creative ways to get information out of his prisoner.

"Crap, Bishop, are you sure this is the best way to get there?" asked Teresa who stood a metre away and held onto the side in the same manner.

"The route Kowalski gave us means we need to change velocity and heading at specific intervals. The normal accelerate, turn and slow down model ain't gonna cut it today. Just listen out for the warning buzzer and hold on. The next change is due in seven minutes."

The route to Prometheus was unlike anything any of them had ever been on before. Both the ship and the computer systems were being pushed to the limits and they were all aware of the danger they would be in if the vessel missed one of the way points by even a few kilometres. As Teresa thought about the route she watched Anderson as he stared at the prisoner. The slender officer looked almost like a schoolboy with his trademark unkempt hair and freckled face. For a second she had doubts about whether he was the right man for a mission like this one. She had seen him in action though and he was easily capable of leadership and violence when the moment called for it.

Teresa placed her hand over her mouth for a moment before straightening up.

"You okay?" asked the Commander.

"I'll live, the trip is a bit rough."

"Watch yourself, throwing up in a vacuum ain't pretty!"

"Thanks, that helps!"

Teresa glared at him and it didn't take long for him to succumb and burst into laughter. The sounds echoed through the open spaces of the ship as it hurtled on its new and uncomfortable route. He pulled out the intercom and hit the general broadcast button.

"Find yourselves somewhere comfortable to hole up, this trip is about to get bumpy."

* * *

Spartan woke to find himself on the floor and with the most outrageous backache. The chamber was bathed in the dull light that their captors considered normal. Most of the other prisoners were stood up, looking around at the fuss in the open space between the cell areas. He started to get up but the pain forced him to stay down for a moment. At first he thought he might be injured but then he remembered the previous night, Misaki jumping on him and then falling to the ground. He moved slowly this time and managed to sit up as the pain started to subside.

"Misaki?" he called, unable to see her.

A siren sound echoed through the chamber and from the right the great shielded door that led back to the surface open to reveal a dozen guards and ten times that number of prisoners.

"Holy shit, man, have you seen this?" asked one of the men.

With a great effort Spartan got to his feet and hobbled over to the large barred doorway to watch the spectacle.

"They're like us, man, just like us!" cried a women in despair as more started shouting.

"Where are they getting them and why isn't somebody doing something about it?"

"Fucking Confed leaving us out here!"

"Hey! What have you done to help the Confederacy other than bitch and whine?" asked Spartan, his blood starting to get fired up. All his life he had heard the whining from bleeding heart liberals about one group being upset or offended but they never seemed to lift a finger to help anyone, except when it made them look good.

"The Confederate military have died in their thousands

to protect people like you. Maybe if more of you had been as angry a few months ago we could have crushed the insurgency and these scum before it got worse!"

The rest of them kept quiet as they continued to watch the scores of people file down into the open space. Just as when they arrived, they started to receive their welcoming speech.

"This room was empty when we arrived, right?" asked the woman, quickly forgetting what Spartan had said.

"Yeah, so?" answered another.

"So if it was empty, were we the first to get here?"

"No. I've spoken to a few people here and this place has been running for months, maybe even years. The last red group must have transferred to the re-education programme or maybe they joined the rest of the prisoners if they weren't strong enough."

"Or they were killed in the sick little arena games of theirs?" came a familiar voice.

Spartan moved towards the sound, past the other prisoners before coming to two men, both seated in the corner.

"Son of a bitch!" Spartan said with obvious pleasure in his voice.

In front of him sat General Rivers and Marcus Keller, his two comrades from Kerberos.

"Spartan, I see you've been pissing off the local girls again?" asked Marcus, the tall, strong looking German.

His family were descended from one of the earliest colonial expeditions to Terra Nova, over three hundred years before. At least that is how he told the story, there were certainly very few German-speaking communities left now.

Spartan turned to his left to see an angry looking Misaki trying to discreetly hide behind one of the other prisoners. He was confused, as he hadn't done anything wrong, to the contrary he had been nothing if noble towards her. He held out his arms towards her, trying to indicate something, anything to her. She recoiled though and shifted back. He sighed and turned back to Marcus.

"Right, you know me. I see you've both got your red armbands, welcome to the club."

General Rivers beckoned for him to sit down next to him on the corner bench.

"I heard they sent you to the Governor. What did you find out?"

"For starters one of the guards did this," he said quietly, showing them his unlocked manacles. "Anyway, the Governor wants military trained people to join their side. He has detailed files on me, I assume he will have the same on you both too."

Marcus looked confused at his comment.

"Don't they already have enough people? From what I've seen the Zealots and their friends already have more than enough people to fight their wars."

"That's what I thought, apparently not though, unless it's just some kind of scam to make us do something. They seem to be collecting people for some kind of epic projects. The only other option is that this is just a glorified extermination camp."

Marcus shook his head.

"No way, man, I ain't going to no bonfire!" he said angrily, shifting from side to side. General Rivers sat listening intently, taking in all the details before speaking.

"What about this red band stuff? One of the women said they put you up against a Biomech? Where the hell did they find those things?"

"Remember the capsules on the ship that brought us here, Sir? They must bring them here for training or something. I don't know, all I know is that they don't seem particularly worried about killing us just as long as enough of us keep working with the labour gangs or fighting their pets."

"I'm sure Confed is doing whatever they can to track us down, what concerns me is that if we didn't know this place existed, then how in the hell will anybody find it now and connect it to our disappearance?"

"You're also assuming they think we are still alive. What if they just said we were executed or died in an accident? Confed has bigger things to worry about right now, Sir."

"Too bloody right it has. Half the colonies have seceded and those that are left are the smallest and least populated in the System. We're gonna need a miracle just to survive this one, let alone actually fight back." Marcus added in a firm tone.

With a familiar sound the barred door slid open to reveal a group of guards. They spoke to one of the prisoners and then escorted him away. This time they didn't leave immediately. The nearest guard spoke first.

"Six more to join your little group," he said as he pushed in another small band of haggard and angry looking people. "I have a have a special message from the Governor."

Reaching inside his combat vest he pulled out a piece of paper and held it in front of him.

"Today you will be split into three groups. Your test will be one of wit and intelligence, as well as strength. The group that takes the least casualties will be offered a place in our re-education programme. The rest will be returned here to await tomorrow's challenge. The groups will consist of those of you with criminal backgrounds in one, Confed personnel in another and the third and final group made up of those of you who don't fit into either group. Remember, we want only the fittest, strongest and most capable in our programme."

The guard put the paper back into his pocket before sliding the barred door shut. One of the new prisoners, a broad shouldered and muscular man grabbed the bars and shouted back.

"Why would I want to join your pissing programme?"

The guard turned back to him. "It's your choice, just remember, nobody lasts more than two weeks in the red group. Do well and get out, or die, that's the choice," he replied before starting to laugh.

The man continued shouting at them but they turned away and walked off to join another group of their comrades.

"Hey!" Spartan tried to gain the attention of the new prisoner.

"What?" barked the man, as he turned and stared back at him, his look was one intended to intimidate but it did nothing of the sort.

Spartan glanced at him, noticing the tattoos running up his arms. On one arm was the Army crest, or at least that is what it looked like from where he was sat. The man was bare-chested and a number of marks and scars indicated either he had a lot of medical work or more likely he was a combat veteran.

"You military?"

"Yeah, Army Alpha Team, why?"

"I thought so, you don't have the brains for the marines!" laughed Spartan.

"Marines?" answered the man with a little disdain before realising he was talking to a marine. The rivalry between the Army, Navy and Marines was well documented and more violent than even that between the Marine Corps units themselves.

"I thought I was the only Confed man here." He marched over and to sit down next to Marcus. As he came closer Spartan could make out the Alpha logo on his bicep. It wasn't a group he knew much about other than that they often competed with the Marine Recon units at some of the inter-service athletic events. At least, that is what he remembered from basic training, it wasn't like he had been in the Corps long enough to participate in anything like that.

"My name's Claus, Corporal 14th Colonial Regiment, Alpha."

"How did you get here?" Marcus asked him.

"We were part of the advanced units deployed on board a suspected hijack near Khimaira. It was a liner, supposedly over three thousand passengers and crew. We boarded the ship and found Zealots in control, about thirty of them. We cleared the decks and regained control of the ship, that's when we found them."

"Found who?" Spartan asked him.

"The passengers. Every single one was inside some kind of liquid capsule. We opened one, the passenger died in less than a minute. I don't know what was going on but there must have been a thousand of them. We hacked the log and the navigation computer to get intel. The ship was being controlled remotely via a computer system but it locked us out before we could get a trace. It seemed they were been shipped off to Orthrus though."

"Orthrus, they seceded along with Kerberos right?" asked Marcus.

"Yeah, well, from what I've heard half the planets in the System have seceded. The video reports we saw said Kerberos, Prime, Orthrus and Agora have all lifted the finger to the Confederacy. That's all the big worlds gone."

"I don't get it, why were they at Khimaira to start with? It's just a gas giant."

General Rivers cut in. "There is more to it than that, Khimaira is surrounded by mining and research stations. In many ways it shares a lot with Prometheus apart from the planet's surface being completely inhospitable. There are platforms in the lower atmosphere, low enough to provide a modicum of gravity, they're more like floating cities than stations."

The soldier appeared more relaxed now as he sat in the company of other veterans. There was something about him though that made Spartan, and to a lesser extent General Rivers, uneasy. Maybe it was just the Army's inbuilt machismo or maybe it was something else. Claus noticed Spartan staring at him and he automatically glared back.

"Hey, haven't I seen you guys before?" he asked as he glanced at the men sideways. Then, as if a light had been flicked on inside his head he recognised Marcus. "Yeah, I know. You're the guys they fingered on Kerberos, for the coup right?"

"Fingered isn't exactly the word I would use."

"Yeah, they fingered us alright, it was a serious set up. We were part of the security detail and tried to stop the massacre. In the end we got framed for the whole thing, why do you think they dumped us here instead of going to trial?" added Spartan.

The group fell silent for a few seconds when the soldier broke the uncomfortable silence. "Whatever, it doesn't really matter now, does it? We're all screwed in this dump!"

General Rivers turned to the bars and looked out into the open area to check what was happening. He had heard several groups being sent out to the work projects but so far none had come back and one should have returned in the last hour. He thought about mentioning it before spotting a small party arriving at the far end. He couldn't see who they were but there were at least twenty of them. He turned back to Claus.

"You didn't say how they caught you?"

The soldier put his chin in his hand for a moment as he thought back to whatever calamity had befallen him. Like the rest of the prisoners they had all experienced a variety of horrors and his must have been of a similar nature. He took a deep breath before turning back to the General.

"It is pretty simple. The escorts for the liner must have been away on another raid because about six hours into our operation we received a distress call from our frigate and then nothing. The bastards must have destroyed her when they came back. All I know is twenty minutes later a dozen gunboats and small vessels docked with the liner and unloaded about a hundred personnel including ten of those Biomechs. You ever fought one of those things?" he asked with a genuine look of horror on his face.

"Yeah, once or twice," said Spartan as he threw a glance over to his comrades.

"We held them for nearly an hour, in the end we were down to side arms when they sent in those things. We tried to hold them off but they are just too much. Only me and one other guy survived, the rest they tore apart, literally before our eyes. They must have knocked us out or drugged us or something, next thing I know I'm being dumped on this rock."

"Same story for all of us then. Where is your partner?"

The soldier shrugged, not answering Marcus, he looked around at the rest of the group and then back to the three men. "So what's the deal then, they interrogating us or something?"

Spartan pointed to a column of about thirty people marching out and towards one of the opening doors.

"Not sure yet. Most of the people coming in are being sent off to work on various projects expanding this place. From what I've seen it is massive, truly massive. They are working on big projects here."

"Like what?"

"Good question, something to do with resources for the enemy. Food, supplies, weapons, equipment or maybe just a simple indoctrination and training centre for new soldiers."

"Like a factory for Zealots?"

"Interesting, it could be or maybe machines or even ships," replied General Rivers.

"Ships? You think they could build something like that and not be noticed?"

"Why not, Claus? They've managed to slip thousands of people off colonies and ships while our forces are busy fighting insurgents throughout the sector," suggested Spartan.

"Yeah, convenient that, ain't it?" said a suspicious Marcus.

The familiar buzz of the cell's door being opened drew their attention back to the newly arrived guards. It was impossible to tell if they were the ones from earlier, apart from slight variations in their sizes they all looked the same. They all wore the same clothing and equipment.

"It is time, come with us." The first guard pointed his rifle at the prisoners.

One by one they marched out until their column moved in the same direction as before. This time their number was larger, bolstered by the new prisoners. As they were leaving two stayed in the cell, one a man in his late forties and a woman in her early twenties who lay down sobbing.

The woman had already survived the first encounter with the Biomechs, but from her reaction she wasn't stable enough to go through the same situation again. One of the guards moved in and pointed his weapon at them.

"Get out, now!"

The two ignored him and stayed still.

"One warning. Either you get out and join them or you suffer punishment!"

The man turned to the guard and took a step towards him. "I don't care! What's the point, we go we die, we stay, we live a bit longer, then die!"

"Not anymore. New rules from the Governor, anybody refusing a direct order is in violation of compound rules and will be transported to the surface, immediately!"

The man started to become agitated, either from the frustration of the situation or because he was trying to get himself to the stage where he was confident enough to attack. The guard must have sensed the danger as he gave a hand signal to one of the other guards who moved up, shotgun at the ready.

"What's it gonna be? Your choice."

The man looked back to the woman who was still sobbing. "You coming or staying?"

The woman sniffed a few times and then stood up. She had the look of someone who had given up thinking and decided to do something. The man looked at her for a moment before looking back to the guards.

"Okay, we're coming," he said and started to walk slowly forwards.

One of the guards kept his weapon trained on the man, the other two stepped back to watch the rest of the group. It was a simple mistake but the price would be deadly. The man had moved no more than three steps when he lunged at the guard. Taken completely by surprise the guard was able to loose off a single gunshot that missed by a wide margin before the man was on him. As the two crashed to the ground the woman screamed and ran towards the fallen pair. Spartan spotted the commotion and tried to move to help but Marcus firmly held him.

"Get back, now!" shouted closest standing guard.

He was already aiming his weapon at the two on the ground but was unable to obtain a clear shot. At the same time the woman rushed forward. It was more a reaction than any kind of aimed shot but the guard easily blasted her with his shotgun. The thermal charge burned through her shoulder and part of her chest, killing her in seconds as she dropped down. On the ground the two men struggled and by some miracle the prisoner was able to draw the man's side arm. With a single shocking blast the round entered the guard's temple at point blank range and sent blood and gore across the floor.

Spartan tried to struggle free but Marcus pointed into the distance at armed men rushing towards them. He was right but it didn't make Spartan feel any better. He wanted to help and he wanted to get off this rock. Six or seven of the group pushed away and grabbed at the nearest guards. One was shot immediately before the closest were overpowered and more weapons taken.

"Take cover!" shouted Marcus as bullets started tearing across the open space between the reinforcements and the struggle outside the cell.

Spartan, Marcus, Claus and Rivers all sheltered down behind the large metal housing near the sliding door. It wasn't a minute too soon either as two rounds struck the thick iron and ricocheted off into the distance. A series of short blasts indicated the rebels had killed the guards on the ground and were now engaged in a deadly firefight. Through the section other prisoners screamed and ran for cover, desperately trying to avoid the crossfire that had already struck two of their number.

"What are we gonna do, man?" shouted Marcus over the sound of the gunfire.

Two more of the rebels were struck down to leave just five who fired from kneeling or standing positions. Double their number of guards moved towards them at a quick walk, their body armour deflecting the odd inaccurate round as they advanced.

"They're getting canned out there. This could be our chance," said Spartan as he pushed away from Marcus.

"Spartan, use your head!" said General Rivers with a stern tone.

"We can do this!" He then rushed out into the open towards where two of the felled fighters lay. One was unarmed but the other carried one of the guard's rifles. It wasn't a model Spartan recognised but it was simple enough. He twisted the safety and aimed at the advancing guards. Remembering his training he exhaled and aimed slightly low. The first round slammed the butt hard into his shoulder and he was surprised at the kick. More importantly though the round had struck the nearest guard in the chest and he was already staggering back. Thinking he might have only a few rounds before they returned their fire, he aimed at the man to the left of the group and then spray a long burst of at least forty rounds before the gun was empty. Two of them managed to reach just a short distance away before the overwhelming fire forced them back. He managed to hit all of the nearest guards, killing three and sending the rest back into cover.

"Jesus Christ, man, you got a death wish or something?" shouted Claus in a mixture of surprise and admiration. "Throw me a piece!"

Spartan kept low and sprinted to the bodies of two of the fallen guards. Both were well armoured though Spartan was a little surprised at the variety of equipment being used. He would have expected more uniformity, not that it mattered right now. Rummaging around he managed to find two shotguns and a pair of pistols. He thrust one into his belt and slid the rest of the weapons across the door to Marcus, Claus and Rivers before pulling himself back into cover. Resting the empty rifle on the floor he pulled out the pistol and slid the magazine out, checking it before slipping around the corner with the pistol drawn and pointing in the direction of the enemy.

Throughout the prison area any of the prisoners who weren't locked away were either cowering behind any cover they could find or running away from the sounds of the battle. The seven remaining guards stayed in their cover though their shooting was sporadic and inaccurate.

"If we're going to do this we'll do it properly, understood?" shouted General Rivers.

Marcus nodded, quickly followed by Claus.

"Spread out, keep low and close the distance. We don't have the time or the ammo for a drawn out fight."

Marcus ducked down and then rushed out into the open and past a group of people hiding behind upturned metal boxes and crates. He dropped down and squeezed off three rounds at the guards before waving for the rest to follow. Spartan spotted two of the guards trying to move back to find better cover and managed to hit one in the leg, forcing him down. His comrade left him bleeding, running back as fast as he could.

"Push them back!" shouted Spartan as he stood from his cover and advanced on the larger group of guards. As they lifted up from cover to shoot he fired single, carefully aimed shots. He wasn't aiming to kill, more aiming to keep them pinned down so they could get closer. He had already covered half the distance before Claus got his hands on another weapon. It was one of the dropped rifles and without hesitating he started to put heavy fire down on the guards. His shooting was fast and precise as another guard quickly went down. As he fell a pair of hands lifted in the air in a plea to surrender, this was quickly followed by the other six. Spartan kept his weapon up high, ready to shoot at a moment's notice and then rushed forwards to the guards. As soon as he reached them he disarmed the first one, taking his rifle, placing his own pistol back in his belt. Marcus moved towards him and did the same. Claus stayed where he was, rifle raised and looking out for signs of the inevitable response by the enemy.

"Don't kill us!" whimpered the nearest guard.

"Kill you, what do you think we are, animals?" asked an angry Marcus.

"Wait, something isn't right." General Rivers moved up, checking the guards. He stopped in front one of them looking at him carefully.

"How long have you been a guard in this place?"

"About an hour."

"What?" Marcus shouted.

"Yeah, I thought so," said the General. "Strip!"

The guards looked at each other in surprise, unsure what to do. Spartan, still not grasping what the General was getting at lifted his own weapon and pointed it at the heads of the nearest two men.

"You heard him!"

The guards needed no further encouragement and quickly started to remove the webbing and armour though in their haste several of them managed to entangle themselves in the gear.

"What the hell?" laughed Marcus at the scene that was rapidly turning to a farce.

As the first man finally removed his body armour the laughing stopped. Underneath he wore prison fatigues and wore the same red band that they wore. Spartan lowered his rifle and walked up closer, holding the arm so that the band was in plain view.

"Why are you wearing this?"

The man started to stutter and Spartan turned his head at a slight angle, evidently unimpressed with the response he was receiving. Two more of the guards had removed their armour and exhibited the same clothing and red bands.

"Look, we're prisoners from the fabrication section. We've been down here for nearly a year. We finished work last week, they said we could join the rest in the factories or do one year's guard work to earn freedom."

"Horseshit, man, no way did that happen!" Claus swore as he moved forward and punched one of the men hard in the stomach.

"Hey, back off, now!" demanded General Rivers.

"Fabrication section, what is that?"

They stood in the centre of the prison compound a number of the prisoners emerged from cover and wandered over to see what was happening. Many more stayed hidden, experience showing them that doing anything other that what they were told usually ended in swift punishment. Misaki stepped forward and bent down, placing her hands on one of the dropped rifles. She lifted it up and pointed it directly at the guards. Her face was contorted with anger and for a second it looked like she was going to open fire on them. Before she was able to make a decision a loud clunk came from the far end of the open hall. Everyone, including the captured guards, turned to the direction of the sound. With a mighty hiss the large metal doors at the end opened to reveal three darkened shapes. They stood there, silent but terrifying as the loudspeaker system switched on.

"This is the Governor, I see you have all been introduced. This is unfortunate but not at all unexpected. Now that you have had your fun all prisoners will return to their holding areas. Guards, return to entry point Bravo for debriefing."

There was a short pause and a number of the people ran back to their cells, some even clambering over the dead or wounded to reach what they considered to be safety. Misaki and two other prisoners stayed out in the open with Spartan and the rest. All were now armed and waiting for something violent and terrible to happen. The speakers clicked once more.

"Of course, anybody refusing to comply will be dealt with in the usual manner, a short visit to the surface." There was a chilled silence, as they all stood waiting.

Almost in perfect synchronisation with his voice the three shapes moved forward to reveal themselves as three-metre tall Biomechs. They were the modified assault troops used so effectively by the Zealots in their struggle against the Confed military. Spartan and his companions, as well as most in the red group, were aware of what they were but many of the others started screaming at the sight of the terrible creatures. They moved to within twenty metres before stopping and lowering their weapons at the group. From this distance they looked like a horrible cross between a human wrestler and an ogre from the old fairy tales. These were no creatures though and were armoured and armed as you would expect to see any other soldier or military vehicle.

"That's just great!" said Spartan in a tone that couldn't have been any less sarcastic.

General Rivers looked around at their small number and then back to the cells where scores of prisoners were cowering.

"What's the plan, General?" Marcus asked him.

The others looked to him as the guards started to move away and towards the doorway. They walked with the obvious body language of defeated men, certainly not the hired thugs they expected would work in a place like this. One of the men stopped and turned back, two of the others stopped with him. He looked about before looking directly at Spartan and the General.

"Did you say General? General Rivers?"

He nodded in reply, saying nothing.

The guard looked at him closely and then over to Spartan, his expression had already changed from earlier, there was now a hint of something. At first glance it appeared to be hope, but closer examination showed it to be more likely intrigue.

"I heard rumours about you, yeah, probably over a year ago. Is it true you held off an insurgent assault on a Confed compound singlehanded?"

General Rivers ignored the waiting Biomechs as he spoke directly to the guards.

"I was the only one left alive, I can tell you that."

The guard looked back at him for a moment and continued his walk to the doorway. For a moment it looked like he would turn back but as he slowed the short figure of Vespis entered, flanked by two armed guards. This time something was different though. Previously the normal security personnel in their dark clothing and body armour flanked him. This time they wore the robes of the Zealots and in Spartan's experience that usually meant lots of additional armour concealed underneath the fabric. Each of the men carried a crude halberd, a polearm weapon with a vicious looking cutting blade and a sharpened tip. As they approached Spartan sensed something had changed and in his experience, it was rarely good.

"You were warned, all of you. You had a chance to get out of here, instead you tried to be smart." Flicking his hand as a signal to the rest of his guards, they each moved off around the group and quickly removed their red arms bands before returning to his side. They were still armed but Vespis didn't seem to be troubled, probably because of his two guards and the three heavily armed Biomechs that watched over them.

"Due to your attempted coup you've been fast tracked to the Harvesting Centre."

"Harvesting Centre?" asked Marcus.

"Are you deaf?" shouted Vespis and with a hand signal one of the guards approached and smashed his rifle into Marcus' stomach. The impact was hard and sent him crashing down to the floor in pain. A spurt of blood gushed from his mouth as he hit the ground. General Rivers bent down to help him but one of the Biomechs pointed a large calibre weapon directly at him and turned its head as if to say no. Spartan glanced at the weapon, noticing it was much bigger than the guns he'd seen them carrying in the past. It was easily the size of a heavy machinegun and contained multiple barrels that presumably rotated around a solid core. He almost forgot their situation as he stared at the new and wicked looking firearm.

"As I was explaining," said Vespis with an irritated tone, "you will be transferred to the Harvesting Centre! It's a nice place, just what people like you need. Somewhere we can make use of those fine muscles of yours!" He looked back to the guards. "Shackle them!"

Spartan moved away from the approaching man. The idea of the Harvesting Centre did little to inspire confidence in his situation. As he started to move he felt the cold metal of a rifle muzzle at his temple. Spartan turned slightly to see it was the guard he had spoken to, he must have turned back to assist in the situation. Vespis moved towards him and gave the guard a harsh look before turning back to Spartan.

"I'm not asking, prisoner. Do as you're told or lose your head, that's your only choice!" he snarled and then moved back to the guard.

"What are you doing back here? You can go back with your comrades for debriefing, then you'll return to your cells. You had your chance!" he snapped.

Three more of the original guards had now moved back near the Biomechs and an argument had erupted though it was too far away for Spartan and his people to hear what was going on. As they stood watching one of the Biomechs twisted its upper body and swung its arm and smashed a guard several metres before he hit the ground. It moved to strike the next man but was grabbed by the other two Biomechs who smashed it down to the floor and tried to hold it down.

"What the hell is going…!" shouted Vespis before Spartan jumped forward and grabbed his left arm, quickly locking his elbow and twisting it behind his back. He screamed out but Spartan forced his knee into the back of Vespis' knee, pushing him to the ground in pain.

Marcus and the General needed no direction and took up positions around Spartan as Misaki stood her ground and lifted her rifle to point at the Biomechs.

"General, now!" shouted the guard who ducked to avoid being struck by one of the Biomechs.

Marcus opened fire first and was joined by the General and Misaki as they poured fire into the two Zealot guards. Their fire was accurate and the first man took the impact of almost fifty rounds in the face and chest. As he hit the floor the second Zealot jumped forward towards them. Several rounds slammed through the robes but must have hit his armour as he kept coming. He reached within three metres of Marcus when Misaki leapt out and smashed the butt of her rifle into his face. As he fell down Marcus put a round into his forehead. The rest of the guards picked up other weapons and signalled to Spartan and the others to join them.

Spartan dragged the still gasping Vespis behind him as he moved towards the fallen Biomech. Around it stood the other two monsters as well as the three guards. The man that seemed to be the leader stepped forward and looked towards Spartan first.

"You can't be Confed military, you move like a pit fighter. What's your name?"

Spartan tilted his head slightly, surprised at the man's comments.

"Spartan."

"Ah, the hero of New Carlos. I've heard of you. Didn't you used to fight in the circuit here?"

"How the hell do you know him?" demanded a less than impressed Marcus.

"I don't know him, I've heard of him," he said before turning back to General Rivers.

"General, we received word almost a month ago they were sending you here. We've been getting ready for six months to get out of this place. We have vital intelligence for the Fleet."

"Fleet? Who the hell are you, son?"

"It doesn't matter, you can call me Tigris. I've been working undercover here since our patrol was captured. We don't have long, are you in, General?"

"We know nothing about you, how can we trust you?"

Vespis started to struggle and Spartan tensed his forearm to pin the man in place as the colour started to drain from his face.

"Look, Sir, I want to get out of here just as much as you do but first we have to shut this place down. You cannot believe what is happening here."

"Why don't you tell us?" suggested Spartan.

The man turned his head in disagreement. "No, no good. You need to see it for yourselves, come on, we need to go."

Spartan shouted to him. "Wait. How can we get out? What about the security system and the guards?"

"We aren't getting out of here, not yet anyway. We can get somewhere safe though and do some damage at the same time," said Tigris.

Spartan looked to General Rivers and Marcus to gauge their thoughts. None of them was particularly happy at the situation but it was better than sitting in the cells waiting to die. General Rivers gave him the nod and then turned to Marcus to whisper something. Spartan looked back to their new allies.

"What about them?" he asked Spartan, pointing to the two Biomechs, as he did they turned and look directly back at him. The nearest turned his head slightly so that one eye stared directly at Spartan's face.

"What about us?" said the creature is a low, growling voice.

Spartan jumped back in surprise and then looked to his right where Marcus and now Misaki stood. They looked equally confused.

"Yeah, good question!" replied Marcus in an almost drunken tone.

CHAPTER EIGHT

The use of kinetic weapons so far after their original development has often been considered one of the failings of the Confederate science programmes. Direct energy weapons systems such as particle beans, plasma weapons and lasers have been in development since the early twentieth century. The greatest obstacles to their widespread use was blooming, high power consumption, beam absorption and the lack of an indirect fire capability.

Experiments with Rayguns

"We have to move now!" shouted Spartan as he helped Rivers drag the wounded guards from the previous firefight into cover along the wall.

Spartan looked back to the large metal doorway about twenty metres away from their position. It was still wide open and on the one side the automated weapon turret sat idly with its glowing eye watching the group. Each of them was careful to not get too close to its cone of fire as like the other weapon systems, its job was to ensure no unauthorised personnel crossed its area of control. On the floor were a series of markings that designated areas that were safe and those watched by the weapon system. There was no way through the door without moving in front of its barrels.

The General himself had already taken a grazing wound to his leg in the firefight. It had been bloody but a quick bandage was all they had time for right now and the injury looked far from critical. As they moved Spartan spotted a Zealot guard taking aim at them. He instinctively pushed the General out of the way and dropped to one knee. As he did he lifted his rifle and fired two aimed shots, both striking the man in the head and neck, forcing him to the floor in agony. Picking himself up he moved back over to the General and continued to help move the injured man.

"Marcus, covering fire, we need to move back!" he shouted.

Tigris meanwhile had managed to sneak up to the control panel and had found the only piece of cover behind the console itself. He was still trying to seal the entry door as Spartan and Marcus fired rapid shots in the direction of the recently arrived reinforcements. As he pressed various buttons, the eye and its attached weapon system panned back and forth as it checked for signs of intruders. They'd already held off one wave in a cunning ambush but their numbers were now starting to tell as more and more of them arrived. It couldn't be long before the Biomechs joined them and then it would be over. Tigris kept hitting a series of buttons but he was getting nowhere. The low pitch tones indicated the system wasn't going to authorise him.

"It's no good, if we can't seal the door we might as well stop now. They will just cut the fans and in a few hours we'll all be dead," said the General as he kept his head down along the sidewall. Each of them was now carrying at least one weapon conveniently taken from the recently killed reinforcements.

Another dozen guards appeared and two of them threw in small metal canisters that clattered around the floor.

"Flash bangs!" shouted Marcus who ducked back.

The rest hadn't time to move and the whole area vanished in a bright white light that rendered them stunned and unable to focus properly. Spartan landed on his back but already he was trying get up up when he spotted the enemy rushing inside. Summoning all the strength he could find he forced himself back up to one knee and lifted his rifle. His eyesight was blurred and his hearing almost non-existent but that didn't stop him from pulling the trigger. It looked like slow motion as the gun jumped and rattled as each round burst from the barrel. The enemy, surprised by the return fire, ducked down and unleashed a devastating amount of fire that forced Spartan to the ground. He rolled over to the left and behind a metal bulkhead off to the side. The enemy must have thought they had killed most of the defenders as they rushed inside the doorway to within just a metre of Spartan. As they moved past he looked over and noticed the General and Marcus were starting to come to, but if he just waited there they would be overrun before they were able to get back into the fight. There was no sign of Tigris and he could only assume he had been killed as the men arrived. Mustering all his strength he pushed himself up.

"Arrgh!" shouted Spartan as he jumped up and hurled himself at the first Zealot guard. The two staggered out into the open but incredibly they managed to stay upright. The others turned in surprise but didn't shoot for fear of striking the guard. Spartan slammed the base of the pistol grip into the man's head and then spun around to fire three bursts into the other men. Two fell to the ground dead but a third managed to avoid being hit and moved ahead to Marcus and Misaki who were still rolling about on the ground. The Zealot stopped and aimed at Misaki's head pulling the trigger but it was too late. One of the Biomechs jumped in the way and took the impact in its chest. It was knocked back a short distance and then aimed its multi-barrelled cannon at the man.

"Die!" it howled in a monstrous roar and fired a long,

savage burst of heavy metal slugs that literally shredded the man before their eyes. Several more Zealots crossed the doorway but were easily cut down by the creature.

Spartan turned back to the man he'd struck who was still moving on the floor. Taking careful aim he fired a single shot into the man's temple, not even hesitating to use his weapon.

"Come on, we can't hold this place forever!" he shouted.

Tigris appeared from behind one of the dead Zealots, somehow he must have ducked away after falling in the skirmish and managed to avoid being hit. He jumped up to the panel and hit a series of buttons.

"No, no way…just give me a…" said Tigris as a high pitch sound emanated from the panel to be followed by the door closing rapidly. As the door shut the lights on the automated weapon systems changed to green.

"Are they off?" asked a surprised Spartan as he pointed at the weapon system.

Tigris nodded.

"How did you know how to do that?"

"A long story, trust me, we don't have time for it, not yet." He moved away from the panel and back to the waiting group of prisoners and guards.

"How long will it hold?"

"The system will rearm in ten minutes providing the correct key is entered and trust me, they have it. This is the only way in from the barracks, we have a really small window if we're going to take it, Spartan."

"What's your plan?"

"We can take the transit corridor to the security room and command centre. If we take that we can access the entire compound's security systems, release the captured ships, the cells and the prisoners. If we're smart we can maybe cause some trouble at the shipyards on our way out."

"Shipyards?" demanded Spartan.

"Like I said, we don't have much time, we should go," said Tigris as he made to move.

"No way, why should we trust you? You've already changed sides, why won't you do it again?"

"Changed sides? I never changed, some of us had to do this to maintain our cover until somebody like you guys came along. Look, you can fly right? And handle a gun? We can't get off this rock without you. Hell, I doubt we'd even be able to breach the security station," he said with an almost pleading expression.

"What about the rest of the prisoners? We can't leave them all behind."

"We won't, but first we have to get to the security room. It's been tried twice before and both times the time sealed locks on the doors opened thirty minutes after an emergency had been declared."

"An emergency?" laughed Marcus.

"Yeah, I think this probably counts!" added Spartan

who was double-checking the magazines he'd taken from the bodies. "I take it when the doors open we'll have everybody here?"

"Yep, and when they get in they won't just punish us, it will be the end for everybody in the cells. They have itchy trigger fingers and aren't afraid to use them. Last time this happened they murdered nearly a thousand people. Most of them forced out on the surface."

"How will we get through the doors to the command room?" asked Spartan.

"Simple," replied Tigris with a hint of a smile. Reaching into his pocket he pulled out his security card. "This little guy will give us access to the security and command rooms, nothing more and nothing less."

General Rivers moved closer and examined the card before nodding in agreement.

"That's all we're going to need. We get to the command centre, open all the weapons stores and release the prisoners."

"Agreed, Sir, come on!" said Tigris as he moved away from the door and rushed along the side of the open space towards one of the armoured and still closed doorways.

"Release them? They'll be massacred!" cried Misaki who until now had stayed silent. She tried to hold Spartan back as he moved past her. He stopped for a moment, looking hard at her.

A small number of no more than a handful of the

prisoners from the red group were still out of their cells and they were already picking up what weapons remained from the battle. One of the men, a gruff looking man in his fifties approached and looked up and down at Spartan.

"What about the rest of them, you're just leaving them here?"

"No, once we have access to the command centre we'll release them. For those that want to fight there'll be weapons, don't worry about that. We need you and anybody else you can find to set up defensive positions in this area until we can get access to the locks for the cells." He placed his hand on the man's shoulder.

"If we don't get back in time we'll need you to hold them off until we can return with more weapons and help free the prisoners."

"I'll stay with them," said General Rivers, " they need someone with experience to hold this place. It's big but there's plenty of cover. If we do it right we could hold back an entire company."

Spartan looked at him but he was less than convinced at the prisoners' ability to defend the place. It didn't matter though as they had little choice. He turned to Misaki.

"Look, Misaki, in the end they are all dead if we don't find a way to escape."

"You're damn right," said the old man as he held his captured shotgun in the air. The man turned and rushed back to the others as he explained the situation. Three of them were already dragging the bodies of those killed to the side of the space for extra cover. Spartan turned back to Misaki.

"It's better for them to die on their feet fighting than on their knees. Come on, we need your help as well!" said Spartan as turned and continued chasing Tigris. Misaki followed close behind.

* * *

Admiral Jarvis stood in the armoured bridge of the heavy cruiser CCS Furious and watched her small armada make slow but steady progress towards its rendezvous with the rest of the Fleet at Khimaira. It had taken some time to finally get this group ready for action. It was only by pressing many of the survivors of the destroyed cruisers at Kronus to serve on the warships, that enough crew had been found to man the vessels. Even so the ships were operating understrength but right now she needed as many major vessels in service as possible. Then of course there was also the problem of abandoned ships that could be used by the enemy. One damaged cruiser had been scuttled at Kerberos already due to lack of resources and to deny her to the enemy. Her armaments and supplies had been split amongst the rest of the ships. The Furious Battlegroup might be at half its normal strength but with four operational ships it would be able to provide a complete and effective combat division for the Fleet.

From the view screen placed inside the bridge she was able to watch a magnified view showing the other ships close enough that she could count the antenna and weapon ports running down the flanks of the massive vessels. None of the ships were in brilliant condition and each was marked and scorched from where they had been sitting for three years in dry dock. They were all Achilles class cruisers, warships designed as flexible ships that could operate independently or as part of a larger group. They were armed in much the same fashion as other Confed capital ships with electromagnetic railguns as the primary weapons. The hulls were littered with point defence turrets and each was capable of carrying a number of shuttles or landing craft. Though unable to deal with something like a battleship they were easily capable of taking on multiple destroyers and frigates or dozens of smaller vessels.

The Furious was something else though. As a heavy cruiser she was a modified and heavily improved Achilles class with additional armour, larger power plant and more powerful weapons. She lacked bays for shuttles to make room for extra armour and gunports making her doubly effective as a weapons platform or command and control ship. She was second only to the handful of battleships and battlecruisers in the sector.

The small task force's destination was the carrier CCS Wasp that waited for the arrival of the Admiral along with a slowly growing number of ships. Since her last visit to Khimaira a month ago the flotilla had increased to double its size and every day more personnel arrived to join the fight. The planet and its orbiting stations had become a kind of rallying point for any forces or vessels sympathetic to the Confederacy.

The communications officer turned in her seat and looked over to the Admiral who was still busy gazing at the assembled ships.

"Admiral, Bellerophon, Patroclus and Perseus report their weapon systems are ready for gunnery trials."

She continued looking out at the ships. Most of the main guns on the cruisers were concealed behind sealed gunports. The design was partially to protect the vulnerable parts of the weapon systems but also to also reduce the warlike look of the vessels when around friendly vessels. It was well known that Perseus had never fired her guns in anger though she doubted that was a condition that was likely to remain for long. Few in the Fleet had managed that luxury in the last months. She barely registered the comments from her officer until noticing her waiting.

"Tell them, good work, they may conduct their drills when ready. I want a full test and evaluation of the sanlav rounds in the cruiser weapons. I expect a full debriefing within the hour," she demanded and then turned to her navigator.

"How long until we reach the Fleet?"

"Twenty-nine hours until Khimaira, Admiral, I've already received word that two more cutters have managed to escape from Orthrus and are due to arrive several hours before us."

"Excellent news, they should have intelligence on the enemies' deployment in that System. Perhaps things are starting to look up for us. At some point the people in the rebel colonies are going to realise they have turned from a fair and equitable system to one of servitude," she said to those on the bridge, though to herself she worried that many might not live to experience the revelation.

"Admiral, we have just received a bounced signal from the Fleet, it is marked for your eyes only from Captain Hardy."

"Put it through to my datapad, Lieutenant."

Admiral Jarvis lifted the device from her belt and waited a few seconds before the encrypted message arrived from her communications officer. It was unusual to receive a message this way she thought. It must be important for it not to go to the commander of the Battlegroup but directly to her. After entering her access codes she accessed the video message. When the access screen slipped away it revealed the face of Captain Hardy.

"Admiral, I have just received an encrypted emergency communication from vessels purporting to be from the Seventh Fleet. The transmission was encrypted but sent to High Command, it contains distress codes and a full log of their transit to our System over the last month."

"Seventh Fleet?" she muttered to herself, "I thought they were part of the Terra Nova Home Fleet. What's going on?"

Admiral Jarvis looked about the bridge, the officers were all busy and the Captain was pre-occupied checking navigation charts. For a moment she considered keeping the information to herself, normally she would discuss this with her right hand man, General Rivers. But with him gone she had no one as reliable and steady as him to talk with. The Captain was a decorated officer with years of combat experience and she had also conducted at least two tours at Carthago in the Alpha System.

"Captain, look at this," she ordered as she lifted her datapad up towards her.

She turned from her duties to the message and read it intently. As her eyes moved further down the page she looked more and more incredulous. When she finished she looked back at the Admiral.

"Interesting. The Seventh Fleet, heart of the Home Fleet. After all this time they just appear, right when we need them. I don't like it, not one bit. This could easily be a trap to lure part of our Fleet to open space to be picked off or attacked. The signal could be faked and we have no idea if there is even a single Confed ship in that area."

The Admiral looked back at the datapad re-reading several of the sections. As she checked the specifics the

Captain brought up a list of known ship dispositions. She centred on the ships known to be part of the Home Fleet. She ran her hand down the list, checking off each of the warships.

"The order of battle at Alpha is impressive, I don't see how a revolt even the size that we have faced could cause much trouble for them. Admiral, do we have any information on what has happened to the Alpha System? Do we assume they are in the same position as us, and trying to regain control? If so why cut off access to us? Maybe they were trying to stop the contagion and revolt from this sector spreading to the home Systems including Terra Nova?" asked Captain Williams.

The Admiral nodded in agreement. She walked to the projection windows looking out into space. One of the cruisers was already firing periodic shots from its starboard batteries into target drones. Some of the weapons were fitted to the rotating sections and others were mounted directly into the static hull behind thick armour. She turned slightly to one side to look back to the Captain.

"That is a good question. The last contact we received told us there had been an attempted coup, almost certainly by forces loyal to the secessionists. It was defeated and an embargo placed on the Proxima System until the situation is resolved. They could quite easily be sat waiting to get the all clear from us first."

Admiral Jarvis walked over to the tactical display and

console and beckoned for the Captain to join her. The display was much like those on board the other capital ships though it lacked some of the three-dimensional display features shown on the carriers and battlecruisers. With a few deft movements she entered her access codes to view the last known Fleet disposition in the Alpha Centauri sector as well as the expected formations and supply routes. The display changed to Alpha Centauri and its two stars. The System was much more substantial and better developed than Proxima Centauri and contained thirteen colonised planets. At the heart of the System was the heavily built up capital of the entire Confederacy, the world of Terra Nova, built in the image of Old Earth and the most important planet next to Prime in Proxima Centauri. The Admiral pointed to a glowing orb in the middle of the map.

"The primary communication hub is based here next to the Alpha transit point and about four days travel from Terra Nova. This is where our signals are normally gathered and then repeated to the various communication channels or ships. We have a similar communication and transit point in this System and yet there has been no communication or travel between them for over three months. The communication routes between the two star Systems had been jammed and the last official contact said they had been struck by a coup attempt and were shutting down the route to avoid contamination. Since then communication has remained jammed with digital noise and no vessels have arrived from Alpha."

"True but with a journey time for manned trips of over three hundred days is that surprising? Even if they left two months ago we would not have seen them yet."

"They could still try to communicate though. All they have to do is get past the jamming at the transit point and they would be clear to transmit. The question is, why haven't they tried?" asked the Admiral.

"Either they are unable to contact us or they are unwilling," explained the Captain.

"According to the attached notes the commander of the group states they are the remnants of a taskforce, including a carrier and a cruiser wing that have survived an ambush on their way from Alpha Centauri to the Titan Naval Station as part of a reinforcement detachment. They have apparently been conducting a fighting withdrawal for the last month. Their ETA at the Proxima transit point is eight days. Thoughts?"

"I don't like it, Admiral, but we can't take chances with something this big. I suggest a token force to meet them. Small and fast just in case they hit trouble."

Admiral Jarvis stood for a moment, considering the situation. The Fleet assembled at Khimaira was closer to the transit point but there appeared to be no great hurry. Vessels could make the journey in two days, more than enough time for her to organise a plan with enough contingencies if it turned sour.

"Lieutenant, get me a secure link to the Wasp, I need to speak with her captain asap."

"Understood," replied Lieutenant Matterson as she started the procedure.

The datapad started to buzz, the familiar sound when a high priority communication had arrived.

"Excuse me," said the Admiral as she moved away to a slightly more discrete part of the bridge.

The incoming message was short but to the point. It was from the Tamarisk that was due to arrive at Prometheus within the hour. They would be making immediate contact with the arms dealer, with the intention of obtaining information to the whereabouts of contraband prisoner transfers and sale. He was requesting any additional units or support Confed might have at the station.

"Good work, Anderson," she said quietly to herself, "with luck you'll find them before they vanish."

A few deft taps on the device and she sketched out an update on the tactical situation near the planet as well as the details of several safe houses if needed. Her final point in the message was that she would arrange for a local team to meet them upon their arrival, details to follow. As she signed out of her device and placed it back in its pouch on her belt, she moved back to her communications officer.

"Almost there, Admiral," said the officer who felt under even more pressure as the Admiral stood patiently.

* * *

They were already through the first door but fierce resistance from the last six remaining guards had kept them pinned down for more than four minutes. The corridor was wide but offered no protection from the defensive fire. The enemy were well equipped with assault rifles and at least one was armed with a thermal shotgun that made a mockery of any kind of armour. One of Tigris' men had already been cut down trying to rush it. Spartan and Tigris kept checking around the corner for an opening but nothing presented itself. The enemy were at the far end where the corridor opened out into a small foyer with what looked like several small blast doors. At least one cabinet had been knocked over to provide the defenders with cover to shoot from.

"We're screwed man!" shouted Marcus, his own weapon now out of ammunition, "I'm out!"

Spartan reached down and pulled his half expended pistol out. He quickly checked the magazine before passing it to Marcus.

"Save the ammo, we need a plan and fast!"

Spartan looked back in the direction they had come from. They'd already killed two guards getting to this stage by rushing the first corridor. The Biomechs had followed them and though one had made it the second had been pinned by a small group of Zealots who had stayed hidden and now cut-off their escape. With time of the essence they had been forced to leave it covering the rear.

"What about him," asked Spartan as he looked towards the waiting Biomech, "can he force his way inside?"

Tigris made to answer but was interrupted by the great beast leaning over and speaking in its gruff, always angry tone. It was well armoured and seemed eager for a fight though whether it could fight its way down such a treacherous space was highly doubtful to Spartan.

"I can do it," it said and without even checking for confirmation it stepped out into the corridor. Bullets struck into its armour immediately but with a series of painful grunts he pushed forward, lowering his heavy Gatling gun and staggered ahead. With a deafening roar the weapon opened up and filled the corridors with flames, smoke and spent shells.

"The crazy bastard!" shouted Spartan. "Follow him!"

Jumping from cover Spartan, Marcus, Tigris and Misaki moved up close behind the hulk. They fired the odd shot past him where they could but his great size blocked most of their view. It took only around twenty steps before they reached the end of the corridor. As the Biomech reached there it staggered and collapsed to the floor, blood dripping from numerous wounds. Spartan leapt over his body and right between two startled Zealot guards.

"Bastards!" he cried as he smashed his rifle butt into the first man's face and then spun around to fire multiple shots into the second who slammed against the wall and then dropped down dead.

Marcus was quickly onto the injured first man smashing his own weapon several times into his face. The next two followed behind and took up positions in case any more guards arrived.

"Inside is the command room, it should be empty, you ready?" asked Tigris.

Spartan nodded and with a firm kick he forced open the unlocked interior door. As he went inside he could see it was empty. The room was about twenty by twenty metres and packed wall to wall with displays and computer systems.

"Jackpot! I'll get the system online, you watch the corridor in case anybody else tries to get in."

"I thought you said that was the only way in?" asked Misaki.

"For us, it is. There are two more access points where the Biomech was killed. If they are fast they could get a few people there in the next few minutes, make sure they don't get in!" he added and then turned to the computers.

"Great work, anything else we might want to know?" demanded an angry Spartan.

Tigris was already hitting buttons on the computer systems and answered but didn't turn away from the displays.

"I doubt it, once I have access you'll have your answers.

Now watch the corridor!"

Spartan turned his head in annoyance. There was nothing he disliked more than when people used him and right now that is exactly how it felt. He waved over to Marcus.

"Back to the corridor, apparently we might be expecting company. Misaki, watch him," he added as he tilted his head in the direction of Tigris.

The two moved back and Spartan tossed her a magazine. At the doorway they came to the bodies of the two Zealot guards and the Biomech who was still moving. Spartan knelt down with a great effort managed to turn it over.

"Spartan!" the creature roared, the pain in its voice evident.

"Hey, easy now, you're badly hurt."

The creature started to make a strange noise and it took a few seconds before Spartan realised it was laughing. The roar was more like a battle cry or howl than anything he had ever heard before. As the creature slowed down its breathing altered slightly.

"Hurt! I will die. Spartan, you must promise!"

Spartan didn't quite hear the last word and leaned in to hear more clearly. As he moved the creature reached out and grabbed him with its muscular arms.

"Promise to release my people!"

Spartan could barely breathe and had to use all his strength to pry its arms from him.

"What do you mean your people? You mean Biomechs like you?"

The creature nodded slowly, blood now dripping from its mouth.

"Release them, give us our revenge!" he snarled and then started to cough blood.

"He's dying," said Marcus.

"Really?" answered Spartan sarcastically.

"Here!" said the Biomech as it lifted its weapon arm to show Spartan his Gatling gun. It was easily as wide as Spartan's head and presumably very heavy. He reached to hold it and as he took some of the weight the Biomech let out a final sigh before becoming still.

"That, I didn't expect," said Marcus as he helped Spartan lower the Biomech's arm.

"Why was he showing you that thing?" he asked as he pointed to the gun.

"He wanted me to have it, to use to free his people. I had no idea they could think or reason for themselves."

"Don't get sentimental on me now, you remember what they did on Prime!"

"True, this one is different though. Look at it, the face is less pronounced and the torso is slightly bigger. Maybe they have been breeding or creating different types."

"What? Like little ones and bigger, tougher ones. Why?"

"I don't know, maybe they haven't perfected the system yet. The first ones I saw when we boarded the ship near Kronus were smaller and faster. They didn't seem particularly intelligent though. This guy could be a new type of heavier, smarter Biomech for a different kind of battlefield use."

As the two looked down at the broken body of the fallen creature the second Biomech arrived.

"Where have you been?" asked Spartan.

The creature looked at him and then down at the body. It could see that Spartan was in the process of removing the gun from the fallen Biomech.

"He was angry, I told him he would die this way," said the creature as it bent down and helped lift the weapon, passing it to Spartan.

Though it was heavy Spartan was strong, well built and used to wielding weapons from his time as a pit fighter. With effort he grabbed the middle section in his left hand and placed his right on the concealed trigger assembly.

"Good. You are like us, you like big guns!" said the creature with what looked like a crooked smile.

Spartan looked back to Marcus who simply shrugged his shoulders. It was a bizarre scene with the three enemies stood in the same place discussing weapons. Spartan noticed a lever on the side of the weapon and tapped it. The barrels started to rotate at high speeds and he had to be careful not to catch his hand in the moving parts.

"They are coming!" said the Biomech as it stepped back and faced one of the blast doors. As it took a few steps back it lifted its arm and the gun on its right arm started to rotate.

"What about the guys back there?" Spartan asked him.

"All dead," came the calm response.

"Marcus, come on, get back!" he shouted and the two men moved taking cover near the doorway that led into the command room. As they took up good positions Spartan glanced back inside to see Tigris still working on the computers.

"Tigris, they're coming. How long?"

"Not long, about another two minutes, you need to hold them back!"

The blast door started to glow along the sides and warmth radiated from the glowing sections. In just seconds large parts of metal were already starting to drip or fall away, then, with a white flash the blast door fell apart to the ground. For a moment nothing happened, smoke and dust scattered from the doorway and then a number of Biomechs, they were the man-sized creatures Spartan had faced on the surface of Prime months earlier. As the first of them leapt inside the entire doorway disappeared in flames from the allied Biomech's Gatling gun. One long burst shredded at least ten of the enemy and cleared the doorway.

"Bloody hell!" Marcus shouted over the din of the weapon.

"It's not like he needs much help from us right now is

it?" laughed Spartan.

As the smoke cleared another mixed group of Biomechs and Zealots appeared and started moving around the doorway but they were obviously unwilling to jump through. One popped his head out and Spartan instinctively hit the fire button on the gun. The recoil was substantial but somewhat mitigated by the weapon's substantial bulk. In less than three seconds he expended hundred of rounds, though whether he managed to hit anything was unknown. He pulled his finger from the trigger and the gun barrel started to slow down.

"Yeah," said the Biomech as it stepped into the doorway and looked out for any sign of the enemy. A few must have caught his eye as he fired two more bursts before stepping back.

"Clear...for now."

The area went quiet, the only sounds the hissing of superheated metal and the groans of several of the dying Zealots. As they stood waiting a low pitched tone echoed through the open space followed by a chorus of clicking.

"What was that?" Spartan called out.

"I've got it, command access to the compound!" replied Tigris excitedly.

Spartan placed his hand on the Biomech's arm.

"Stay here, I'll be back." He rushed back inside the room. Tigris was already moving scores of video screens about on the displays.

"What do you have?"

"What don't I have?"

Spartan looked unimpressed and moved his hand to touch one of the displays.

"Hey, uh, don't touch that. Look, I've released the locks on the cells, every single cell in the place. That's your block plus the other fourteen of them."

"Fourteen? There must be thousands of prisoners here?" Misaki said in surprise.

"At least. The security system is offline and I've triggered a system reboot which will take up to an hour before everything else comes back. After that the doors, locks and guns will come back under the control of the supervisor of the system."

"Who is that?"

"That's the problem, the default system supervisor is the Governor."

"So what are our options?"

"It's quite simple, Spartan, either we use the time we have to get out of this place or we try and take over the entire compound."

"How could we get away? By ship?"

"Good question, Misaki."

With a few deft hand movements he brought up two video feeds that showed massive caverns full of people working and vast structures surrounded by scaffolding and machines.

"What is that?"

"The shipyards. I told you, Spartan. These guys have been working here for sometime. They've been launching one every month since I've been here."

"That doesn't help us though, what about operational vessels, is there anything we can use to escape?"

"I'll check," he said as he looked through different feeds.

Spartan looked at the feeds before looking down at the gun he was still carrying. He thought back to the dead Biomech and what it had said.

"The Biomechs, why did they help you?"

"I managed to alter the programming on a dozen of the capsules in the new chamber that was being constructed during the last breakout attempt. It might have failed but it gave me the cover I needed to make the changes. I disabled the indoctrination program they've been running so when the Biomechs were released three weeks ago they were screwed up. They must have thought they were faulty because they were used as cannon fodder in the arena or for training the other Biomechs. Shame I couldn't do any more, but when the revolt failed I had to get back and help round them up or they'd know something was up."

A red light started flashing on the panel and on one of the screens an incoming message alert appeared. Some of the camera feeds started to shut down and Tigris tapped furiously on the virtual keyboard as he managed to lock out parts of the system before control was removed.

"What is that?" asked Marcus.

"It looks like several ships have just taken up positions over the compound. One of them is trying to obtain remote access to the security system. They managed to get part of it, including access to the outer door and the shipyards, but I've managed to lock down the rest."

"Good work."

"Yeah, I take it this scuppers our escape plan though? No point trying to escape in a transport when they have ships waiting for us."

"God, Spartan!" Misaki called as she gazed at one of the screens.

"What is it?"

"No way, look," said Marcus as he leaned closer to one of the displays.

"Here, let me," said Tigris as he moved the video feeds to a series of larger displays that were mounted in the freestanding wall in the middle of the room. The first screen showed a long hall easily up to a kilometre long. It was packed full of cylinders just like the ones on the ship that brought Spartan and his comrades to Prometheus. That wasn't the image that had caught Misaki's eye though. It was another area, much smaller, where bodies were being loaded onto conveyer belts by large numbers of people. As Spartan watched he followed the body of a man as it worked its way along the belt before reaching a large metal box where it subsequently disappeared.

"God, what is this place?" demanded Spartan.

"I told you, this is the Harvesting Centre. It's where they take the strongest prisoners. The machines harvest bodies, tissue and organs to make and repair their new toys."

"Toys, you mean the Biomechs?"

"Yeah, exactly. This is where they make them. From what we've worked out they modify the strongest prisoners, like your red group, with equipment in the factory rooms. Tissue, organs and other stuff like that goes to the same place. All I know is that people and body parts go in one end and at the other we get creatures like him." He pointed to the doorway where the Biomech stood, waiting patiently with its gun.

"But how many are they making?"

"Marcus, thousands from what I can see."

Spartan was deep in thought, busy scratching his chin before interrupting them.

"Hang on, how long does the indoctrination program take to change them?"

"A few days I guess, why?" asked a confused looking Tigris.

"Because if we can free them we'll have thousands of Biomechs who I'm sure would very much like to know what has been going on."

"Spartan, are you serious? These things have killed

thousands already," exclaimed an angry Marcus.

"Yeah, that's exactly what I'm talking about. They are intelligent creatures, just like us. The ones we've fought were tortured, mind altered and savage. We can turn them into an army, maybe even allies! We certainly have a shared enemy."

They all went quiet for a moment as they tried to absorb the revelations and possibilities they had discovered. The light on the console kept flashing red, reminding them of the circling enemy vessels.

"Spartan, I like it, what's your plan?" asked a pleased looking Misaki.

CHAPTER NINE

Private spaceflight is now a common occurrence with both private enterprise and even some wealthy individuals now being able to take part in space travel and commercial ventures away from their home worlds. The first of these ventures occurred in the late 20th century where wealthy donors could hitch rides on national space programmes for a fee. This expanded rapidly into the 21st century with the rise of space tourism. The following decades moved quickly to commercial exploitation of the resources around Old Earth. Once the first interplanetary colonies were formed it would never be the same again.

Origins of Private Space Travel

Bishop took his rifle apart for the second time in the last hour. Working on equipment in a zero g environment was certainly different to when he practiced on the base, but there were benefits. Providing the vessel was coasting, as it was right now, there was no gravity and the parts stayed roughly where he left them. One game he and Kowalski played was the thirty-seconds weapon strip. If they were fast enough the parts would stay close enough to the starting positions and the job could be done without placing them on any magnetised surfaces. Right now though he was taking just one part off at a time, cleaning and checking for any imperfection or dirt that might impact on its effectiveness. It wasn't really necessary, the weapons were all in a state of excellent condition but it gave him something, anything, to do while they waited for the last six hours of their trip to come to an end.

They had left the outer reaches of the storm areas over an hour earlier but travelling any faster in this region would draw attention to them in a very busy shipping area. Not that Bishop was complaining, the journey through the storms had been horrendous and the ship had sustained damaged to one if its engines on the tail end of the trip. He was just thankful they managed to make it without losing any major systems or taking damage to the habitation sections.

As he placed the barrel back into its housing he checked one of the monitors that watched the exterior of the ship. From this position he counted at least ten large vessels, cargo ships and transports each the size of a Confed battleship. Scores of flickering lights indicated the myriad of smaller craft as they moved about their business carrying people and supplies throughout the stations, bases and planetary compounds. It was much busier than he had ever expected.

"Bishop, double-check the weapon housings. It is imperative that nothing can be detected from our containers. If they pick up the firepower in this ship we'll be intercepted by customs and checked, then we'll be screwed."

Bishop snapped the separate parts of his rifle mechanism back together with a satisfying clunk and then placed it on one of the many clip mounts on the walls of the room. He then reached out to the intercom on the wall near to where he was working.

"Roger, checking now, Sir."

He pulled himself out towards the access door to the spinal corridor that ran the length of the ship, stopping at the engineering panel. With a few deft taps he switched to the weapon maintenance panel that was retrofitted when the ship had been rebuilt and heavily modified.

In the main habitation section of the ship Kowalski and Commander Anderson made their own final checks as they moved ever closer to the Prometheus Trading Post. Most of the computer displays showed columns of details and figures on the state of the fuel and their flight trajectories. Anderson leaned back, so far it all looked good. That was something that always worried him.

"Sir, we're picking up a coded message from the station, are we expected?" asked Kowalski as he rechecked the signal for authenticity.

Anderson moved up to the communications unit to check the details himself.

"It looks okay, the watermark and sig file are all current. Audio or video?"

Kowalski split the incoming data streams up so that he could remove the content from the secure packets. It took only a few seconds as the computer checked the data for errors or security problems before it could be viewed.

"It's a live video stream, Commander, shall I connect and respond?"

"Negative, put the stream on the board, let's see who we are dealing with first."

As Kowalski moved the live stream to the larger display, with surprising speed an image appeared of a small room, though the subject in the middle was just a shadow. Kowalski turned up the brightness and adjusted other colour levels until they could see it was a man in a dark room speaking directly into a microphone. No matter what he changed he couldn't get any more definition other than a basic outline of the man.

"Tamarisk. Good to see you arrived safe and sound from your hazardous trip. I trust all went well. My name is Angelo, I'm part of a recruitment agency on Prometheus Seven, I specialise in assembling problem solvers with specific skills in a very short time. I've been contacted by our mutual friend Ganymede concerning your personnel requirements and have been informed of your operational needs and tight deadline. Please respond."

"What the hell is that all about?"

"Sounds like code to me," said Teresa as she arrived in the cramped room, gently pulling herself along with the grab rails and placing a hand onto Kowalski's shoulder. He jumped at the unexpected contact.

"You're right," replied Commander Anderson. "I've not heard of Angelo before, but single name units are almost black ops of some kind. Ganymede is the codename for command officers of Admiral or higher."

"Man, I hate it when you sneak up like that!" said a shaken Kowalski.

"You need to chill out, Kowalski, it's only me!" she replied with a grin.

"Okay, this looks safe to me. Establish a comms link with this character and set our transmission to audio only, no reason to give him a free look at us."

"On it, Sir."

"This is Tamarisk, we weren't expecting any assistance," said Commander Anderson.

There was a short pause as they sat waiting before the man in the video appeared to nod and then started to speak.

"I was contacted recently by a mutual friend. She said

you might need assistance of the physical kind upon getting here. I've taken the liberty of assembling a team of locals. The price wasn't cheap but the bill has been covered by Ganymede."

The Commander hit the mute button and turned to Kowalski and Teresa.

"He said she, it could be the Admiral."

"Makes sense, she's the only senior commander with full knowledge of our mission and she knows we are due to arrive soon. Can we trust them?" asked Teresa.

The Commander shrugged and turned back, releasing the mute key.

"We are due to land within the hour at Docking Bay 14, we'll meet you there," said Anderson immediately cutting off the sound. They sat and waited before a final message came back.

"Understood, Tamarisk, safe journey, we will see you shortly, out."

The video cut to black and was quickly followed by a connection terminated message.

"Do we need their help, Sir?"

"No idea, Teresa, but if we need to break into a prison facility or ship we'll need every hand and weapon we can find. If it was indeed the Admiral then she will have arranged the best she can find at such short notice."

"Who are they anyway?" asked Kowalski who turned away from the computer for the first time in the last hour.

"The Confederacy has Black Ops units throughout the sector. Some gather intelligence, others are sleepers who wait for orders as and when they are needed. My guess is this Angelo is part of an Intel team out here. Lots of information, goods and money pass through this area all the time. As for the people he has assembled, well, they will almost certainly be local mercs."

Kowalski scratched his neck and appeared lost in thought before speaking again. "Mercs, out here? I thought the Confederacy stopped using hired guns decades ago."

"Officially we stopped the mercenary units being used in the Army. After all, why pay for mercs when you can get professionals for less money and without the loyalty issues. They do have their place though, especially when you need a proxy."

"Proxy? What do you mean?"

"He means, Teresa, you pay somebody else to do your dirty work. It costs a bit more but if it goes wrong you don't take the heat," replied Kowalski.

"Yeah, something like that. Okay, this is going to be interesting. I want all of you to re-read the files on the station and on our contact. We will be there in fifty minutes and I don't want to be caught with my trousers down. Don't forget, we are black market traders looking to buy weapons and armour for insurgents. Keep quiet, be discreet and for God's sake don't call me Commander. Understood?"

Teresa and Kowalski both nodded, Bishop shouted back down through the ship to acknowledge the plan.

* * *

The series of vertical display units showed feeds from more than twenty locations in the facility. On three of the screens were scores of guards, each collecting equipment from the barracks and assembling at two open areas near the building. One display showed a massive computer centre that must have been at least a hundred square metres, packed with large metal units and cooling systems. The other displays showed hundreds of prisoners rushing from their cells. Some were overpowering their guards, others grabbing captured equipment, many more simply cowered or hid as they waited for whatever unfortunate event was about to unfold.

"We're going to have to get this thing organised. Once the guards enter the main areas they will have co-ordination and firepower on their side."

"The prisoners won't stand a chance, Tigris. We need to even the odds somehow. What exactly do we have access to here?" asked Spartan.

"Well, when the ships arrived they were able to connect to and access the mainframe, wherever the hell it is. They shut off access to the management and computers systems as well as the communications gear. We've still got control over the security systems, ventilation and cells, that's it though. We can't do anything to the harvesting areas, shipyards or anything outside the compound."

"What the hell?" Marcus paced back and forth like a caged animal, muttering to himself.

"This isn't good. So all we can do is release the prisoners and give them access to most of the base. Is there nothing else we can do from here? What about the Biomechs? Can you change their programming, maybe get them to help in the fight?" asked a despondent Spartan.

"No, not from here, that has to be done at the actual location where the Biomechs are being made. Also, it doesn't take minutes. The changed programming could take days to kick in for the newest models and the older ones will take even longer. We don't have the time right now, why change them if we'll be dead within the hour?" answered Tigris as he turned back to the displays that were still functional, for signs of anything that could help them.

"What do you know about this computer area here?"

"No idea, Spartan, I've not seen it before. It must be important though, look at the cabling on the base layout and the power management. Holy crap, it is big!" said Tigris as he scrolled through several diagrams.

"Hey, I recognise that layout." Misaki stepped closer. She examined the details and then checked two of the displays where the metal housings hid the cables from the computer area. She started to nod the more she looked.

"Well, what is it?" asked Marcus.

"When we arrived I noticed a large communications tower. It was the only substantial structure in this entire area on the surface. Those containers and housings run from the tower down to the computer centre. If you look here you can see smaller communication connections moving out to the factories, harvesting areas and shipyards."

"So you're saying this computer system is networked throughout the compound, so what?"

"No, that's not what she's saying, Marcus," said Tigris, who looked as though he had already worked it all out. He pressed a few buttons and brought up the network details for the entire system. "The bulk of the data and computer power is being moved between this centre and the communication tower. If you ask me this entire facility is being controlled or managed from elsewhere."

"What about the Governor then?"

"He's a brute and a bully, Marcus, but he doesn't look like the kind of man who could manage and operate a complex facility like this. Tigris, if you're right then somewhere in this sector is a base or hub that controls it," Spartan added as he stood at the sector map that showed the planets, stations and steroid belts that littered the Proxima Sector.

"Not just this place, Spartan, it could control many more, possibly dozens of them through Proxima Centauri," Tigris said as he traced his fingers across a number of the planets.

"You know what you're saying, Tigris? The Zealots and their partners could just be the tip of the iceberg with this thing. They could have thousands more Biomechs, maybe even ships being hidden away, ready for the moment to strike."

Spartan thought for a moment and continued, "This is all speculation but if, and this is a big if, this station is one of many and it is being controlled from elsewhere then we have a duty to get the information out of here. Even if we don't get off this rock, people will have to know."

"Are you saying what I think you're saying?" Marcus asked.

Misaki raised her eyebrows, desperately wanting to know what they were talking about.

"We need to control that communications tower so we can get a signal out to warn the Admiral and anybody else who is listening. There is a sickness down here, something dark and dangerous and I think Confed are going to want to hear about it."

"I've got an even better idea," said Tigris. He pressed three buttons and brought up the images of the prisoners in one of the sectors where they were engaged in bloody fighting with a small number of guards. "What do you think the public would think if we could show them pictures of this? Video footage of the prisoners, the guards, the labs and the Biomechs being built here from the flesh and blood of our own people."

Spartan nodded with a wry grin. "Tigris, now you're thinking like an officer. Turn the population against their masters."

"Okay then, what do we need to do?" Marcus asked.

"Tigris, somehow I don't think they are just going to let us walk into that place and start using their system. Also, when they realise what we're doing won't they just destroy the communications gear?"

"Time isn't so much the problem, Spartan. As long as we can get a data packet out of this area I can lock onto any repeater stations in orbit around the planet. If we can transmit a general distress for up to a minute it will propagate throughout the network on the public channels."

"Are you sure, Tigris?" asked Misaki.

"What's the point of a clear, unencrypted data channel if you can't transmit to it in an emergency? That's why we have it! But we need to hit the computer centre and fast, before they get there first."

Tigris brought up the map to the compound centred on their position in the security room. The site had the look of a spider with them positioned halfway along on the left. Four of the legs were fitted out with harvesting rooms, prison cells and at the tip were the shipyards. Another four arms were in various states of completion. Tigris traced his hand from the tip of their leg on the base.

"So this is where we all arrived. Each end of the leg section leads to the surface where the loading bays, platforms and hangars. As you move in you come to the prison cells and the barracks. Now there is one barrack building per leg. We've been fighting one of them so far. If you move further along the leg it gets wider till you reach the centre."

"What's in the middle?" asked Spartan.

"The harvesting areas and shipyards are based around the wide sections of each leg where it joins the central hub. The main office for the Governor is here, at the end of our leg."

"Why isn't he in the middle?"

"I don't know, good question, Marcus. I've only seen a small part of this myself. I might have been a guard but they never trusted us with more than one sector."

Misaki moved the map to get a closer look at the central hub. She zoomed in to examine the shafts, corridors and rooms. "Okay, it looks like the computer centre is right in the middle, further below the surface than any other part of the base. Why? Don't computers usually go further away from heat?"

"Could be using the thermal energy to power the place. Also, don't forget if this place is as heavily protected and controlled from elsewhere you're going to want the computer gear as far away from the surface and interruption as possible," said Spartan. Misaki looked back to the map and continued.

"If you move up you'll come to the large barracks structure. Above that, right on the surface is a massive open area with access doors leading to the surface."

Tigris leaned in and quickly spotted the obvious.

"They are for launching ships when they are completed in the shipyards I would think. Look, the route from the yards is short and direct, right to the surface."

"The route from here to the computer centre leads right past more prison blocks, then the barracks before we get to the security gate here. We'd have to reach it, defeat or bypass the guards and then smash the gate to reach the elevators to the centre," said Spartan, partly to himself and also to the group.

"No, the elevators are out as long as the security system is down. It's all part of the system."

A loud thumping sound came from the corridor and they all turned as the Biomech lumbered inside. The creature looked bored, it had been stood in the corridor for some time now as they went over what to do. It glanced at each of them and then at the screen before turning to Spartan.

"Well?"

"We're going to show everyone what is happening down here. When we've done that we're freeing your friends from these bastards!" said Spartan firmly.

"Good!" growled the creature with a satisfied expression

on its face.

"What's your name?" asked Misaki.

"Name? We have no names," it replied in a monotone voice.

Spartan moved up to him and looked carefully at the creature's face. "Yeah, he has a name, look at him. He's a crazy bastard, just like me!"

"Well?" asked Misaki impatiently. Spartan turned back to look at her.

"Gun."

Marcus shook his head at the idea.

"Gun?" asked the creature before looking back to Spartan. It lifted its arm to show him the Gatling gun.

"Yes, Gun!" he growled with obvious pleasure.

* * *

The Tamarisk sat on the landing pad, its legs extended to support the vast bulk of the vessel. Most stations would be unable to house such a craft but this Prometheus Trading Station was one of the largest manmade structures in the entire Confederacy. At the bottom of the ramp Commander Anderson, Bishop and Teresa stood waiting. Kowalski stayed behind on the ship in case of trouble and to man the ship's weapons in case they needed to make a hasty retreat.

"Where are they? We're in the right place?" asked

Teresa.

Bishop checked his datapad confirming the landing spot was to be Bay 14. He looked up and spotted the peeling red paint up on the wall. "Look, like I said, 14, we're in the right place."

Almost on cue the circular door leading away from the landing platform hissed open to reveal two men, one in a scruffy leather jacket and a pair of faded combat fatigues, the other in a cheap suit. Both walked up to them and stopped three metres away. The man in the leather jacket moved ahead slightly.

"I'm Angelo, this is my associate Mr Jones who resides on this station."

"I'm Ter..." started Teresa before the man raised his hand and cut her off.

"Please, no names here. I know who you are and you know more than enough about me already. If you're ready I have somewhere a little more private where you can meet the rest of the group and let me know about the plan. Are you ready?"

Commander Anderson nodded. "We're ready."

"Good. Let's go," said Angelo who then turned and walked back through the doorway, closely followed by the man in the suit. Commander Anderson moved up behind with the other two following. Bishop tapped him gently on the shoulder as they were leaving.

"The plan?" he asked quietly.

"Yeah, we'll think about that when we have information from Hex. Just play along." Bishop turned to Teresa who was leaning in to listen.

"It just keeps getting better and better doesn't it?" he said with a grin.

"Great," replied Teresa as she slid her hand away from the concealed pistol tucked inside her jacket.

They went though the doorway and into a small arrivals lounge. It was obviously well used by traders and travellers rather than tourists or more important personnel. The walls were worn, the interior was shabby and grimy. As they carried on Angelo turned his head to speak to them.

"It doesn't look much but this is the quietest part of the station. There are more salubrious places of course," he explained and gestured off to a set of airlock doors to the right. "You first."

Teresa and Bishop walked up to the door as it opened automatically. They felt a subtle but noticeable difference in air pressure and temperature. Inside was a circular room with a high ceiling and many reflective surfaces. In the middle was a water feature that babbled away into a small recessed pond. Teresa went through the door and stayed close to the wall. As she moved slowly along the perimeter Bishop came in and did the same on the other side. Angelo nodded and indicated for Commander Anderson to enter. He paused for a moment before stepping through the entrance, the rest followed closely behind.

"Interesting place you have here," said Anderson as the door slid behind them. As it shut the room must have pressurised as he could feel a slight change in his ears.

"Just wait a moment," said Angelo as he stood still.

A barely audible clunk echoed through the room that was followed by a low level hum.

"We are clear now, please, have a seat," he said pointing to the green chairs that were scattered about the place.

The water in the middle of the room continued to fall and that, along with the odd hum and air pressure, made all three of the crew feel uneasy.

"It's no big deal. This is our meeting room, it is ionized and cleansed by our scrubbers, we have sensors throughout and the water helps as an audio screen. It is almost impossible to bug this place," explained Angelo.

Commander Anderson sat down and beckoned for Teresa and Bishop to do the same. As they did so Angelo and the man in the suit did as well. With the five of them seated Angelo spoke first.

"Please, no names, even here. Understood?"

Anderson and the rest nodded in agreement and it looked like Anderson was going to speak first before Angelo beat him to it.

"I have been monitoring traffic in this System for the past three weeks and there are a few anomalies that might be of interest you and your business here. Before we start though I assume you are familiar with the situation here?"

Before anybody could speak the man in the suit explained.

"You should know that this System is not easy to reach so when people do get here they tend to stay for some time. We have a lot of traffic between the planet, research labs, factories, quarries, stations and the like. So much that we have no adequate way of monitoring what goes on here. On top of this the locals are hostile to any external influences on what they do. There are literally hundreds of organisations and corporations with a vested interest in this System and all of them make use of private security. You can't even visit a factory or planetary mining facility without a dozen guns pointing at you. I assume you are aware of the high levels of drug trafficking here as well as slavers, prostitution and unregulated fighting?"

"Let me stop you there," said an irritable Anderson. "We've been here before and we're well aware of the undesirable nature of this place. That isn't why we are here now. What do you know about us and are there anomalies?"

Angelo nodded with a slight smile coming to his face.

"Good, I heard you were a man of action, not words."

He reached down and pulled out a small device about the size of his hand. Laying it out in front of him it flickered several times before showing a holographic model of the station.

"First of all I know you are here to find someone, the

trouble is so is everybody else. In the last three weeks the amount of external traffic has increased by two hundred per cent. That isn't the real deal though, what interests me is that most of the new traffic is coming right through the storms."

"I thought the storms were dangerous?" asked Bishop, trying to sound innocent. Commander Anderson threw him a look that told him to keep his mouth shut.

"Quite. The current reports show over a dozen ships have been lost in the last five days alone. Somebody it seems really wants to move something back and forth and they aren't worried about the risks. All that to change the flight time to weeks instead of months. Would you know anything about that?"

Commander Anderson shrugged, saying nothing.

"I see. Well, as far as what you wanted done here I have a number of people on retainer that can be assembled within the hour."

"What kind of people?"

"Engineers, technicians, security specialists, pilots... useful people. I've been instructed by Ganymede to make my full dossiers available for your perusal," he said with a look of interest in his face.

"Good, for now we have an operation on this station to attend to. The matter of the arms fair."

"Ah, yes, I have secured access for the three of you to visit in the next thirty minutes. Your details are already logged under the name of your trade ship Tamarisk."

"They know our ship?" demanded Teresa.

"Of course, all vessels docking or landing at stations will be logged. It is always easier to hide something in plain sight."

"How about you? Are you coming?" she asked him.

"No, I'm already known to several of the buyers that might be there. I will be on standby at this frequency. Use the access codes I attached with the communication earlier. When do you plan on attending the fair?"

"Immediately, we can't afford to lose any time," said Anderson as he made to move.

"Before you go it's important that you understand the people you will be dealing with. From my sources I already know two of them are selling weapons to the drug Cartels on the Rim and one is a known cop killer from Kerberos. Don't kid around with them, they play tough and they act tougher," he said seriously.

"Don't worry, we can handle ourselves," replied Teresa as she stood up.

The man in the suit beckoned for them to wait a little longer.

"This particular arms fair is specifically personal firearms, especially those of a more unusual and specialist nature."

"Unusual, you mean illegal?" asked Teresa.

"Of course, you won't find much in the way of legal

civilian weapons there. So don't make a fuss when you spot gear that has been taken from Confed stores. There's a lot of cachet to making use of stolen military gear. The Black Blades Gang on this station was famous for all using Confed Army issue pistols and blades."

"Yeah, made it easy to track them though," Angelo interrupted.

"To get there taken the elevator to the fifteenth level, you will exit from the service shaft into the back section of the main foyer. It is always very busy, watch for pickpockets and head to the main desks. Above the desks are the screens for conferences, meetings, demonstrations and the like. You are looking for the Tactical Gear and Supplies Fair."

Bishop and Teresa looked at each other in confusion.

"Don't worry, it's just a simple cover for the main event. When you arrive you will need to ask for the 'specials'. That will get you into the more exotic line-up of kit. After that you're on your own. Remember, there are no police out here. The Trading Station has its own security personnel and they always, and I mean always, come down on the side of those with the biggest wallet."

Commander Anderson stood up and headed to the door. Teresa and Bishop were close behind him. Angelo stood up and watched them leaving the room.

"My associate will be here if you need us, you have my details, just be cool. I'll make sure the team is ready for your inspection. Good luck."

As they left the door shut behind them leaving the three out in the quiet, slightly damp corridor. There were only two directions they could take, either left to where they had landed or right that led further inside the station.

"Ready?" asked the Commander.

Bishop nodded as Teresa checked her pistol was in position before confirming.

"You only brought the synthetic, right?" he asked her.

"Yeah, and she's loaded with plastics only."

"It's time for you to hide it somewhere discreet."

"Don't worry, they'll have to get real friendly to find it," she said with a smile.

Anderson grinned and then turned to check their route. "It's time then, let's go."

They moved off at a fast walk along the corridor, the Commander at the front and Teresa at the rear. Though they moved quickly they didn't want to arouse suspicion if anybody was watching. It took less than a minute for them to reach the end where they met three doors. Two were locked and presumably store or control rooms. The third door was wider than the others and fitted out with a keypad and display. As Bishop moved closer it must have detected his position as the display altered to a rough outline of a face.

"Please enter your destination," it asked in an artificial and less than friendly voice.

"Charming," said Teresa as she glanced at Bishop.

"Let me," said Commander Anderson as he leaned in and pressed the one and the five. As soon as he moved his hand away the door slipped to the side to reveal a small metal elevator. Teresa went in without a thought, quickly followed by Anderson. As they turned Teresa noticed Bishop was still outside.

"What?"

Bishop took a breath and then stepped in. As the door shut the display starting counting the floors as they were whisked to their destination.

"What was that all about?"

"I had an, well, a problem in one of them years ago, Sir. It was stuck for over a day and started to drop. I've never trusted them since."

"Don't worry, if it really breaks you'll be a dead man anyway!" laughed Teresa.

"You ever been here, Teresa?"

"No, Sir, this place was always a bit too upmarket back in my day."

"Upmarket? You kidding me?" asked a less than sympathetic Bishop.

The elevator made a curious whistling noise as it travelled through its tight fitting tube. After a few more seconds it started to slow and with a slight jolt stopped.

"Floor 15, Main Foyer," said the computer as the door opened.

Directly in front was the massive entrance to the trading station and it was already clear the entrance was designed to impress. Apart from a vast circular floor there were three spiral staircases winding around what appeared to be a statue of a man planting a tool of some kind into the ground. Scores of large displays, many over five metres high, pushed up from the ground and around them hundreds of people moved about. Many rushing about their business, the rest gazed intently at the information being provided.

"Wow, nice digs," said Bishop.

"Yeah, wonderful," said Teresa as she scanned from left to right. "There, the desks, we need the route to the place."

They made their way across the crowded foyer. As they walked Bishop was amazed at the variety of people. Some were just workers but there were also mercenaries walking about in full army issue carapace armour. As two walked past he tapped Teresa on the shoulder. She tilted her head slightly, watching them.

"I know, remember what Angelo said about the weapons and security."

They continued on past the people until they were close enough to the desks to see the screens above them. There were eight desks and each one carried two displays overhead. Anderson waved for Bishop to take the ones to his left. Teresa did the same to the right and she spotted the fair almost immediately.

"Look, we take the route past the stairs, through the doors and then follow the red line till we reach the convention reception."

Anderson nodded in satisfaction and pointed in the direction they needed to go.

"Shall we?" he asked rhetorically.

They left the desks and moved past the staircase. It was less busy along this part of the foyer but there were still a lot of people milling about. As they reached the doors a man in an armoured suit and carrying a box on his shoulder walked towards them. As they went to go through the doorway he turned and glanced at them.

"Arms Fair?" he asked.

Teresa looked to Anderson who simply nodded.

"Don't bother, you're too late now. Something's going on down there and they're kicking customers out," he said and then continued on his way.

"What the hell?" called Bishop before turning and running down the corridor. Commander Anderson tried to grab his attention but he was already around the corner. Teresa looked to him before he gave her the nod. They ran the short distance to find Bishop and about a dozen irritable people milling about outside the entrance to the convention centre. Bishop stood there shaking his head as Anderson walked up to the two mercenaries who were guarding the doorway. He was about to speak when two men and a woman in white overalls, and the symbols of the Prometheus Emergency Clinic, emerged pulling a wheeled stretcher out of the room. On top was a covered object, presumably a body.

"You've got to be kidding me?" said Teresa quietly to herself.

Anderson stepped aside to let the medical personnel pass him, before moving closer to the guards. As he approached he noticed one of them moving his hand down to a weapon on his belt. Anderson made sure he kept his hands in plain sight, directly in front of him.

"What's going on?" he asked.

"Who knows, we opened for viewings ten minutes ago and that's when we found him."

"Are you going to re-open?"

"No, the fair is shut till tomorrow, the investigators will need time with this one. Why, who are you after?"

"Maximilian Hex, we have an appointment," replied Commander Anderson.

"Had, I think you'll find is the correct syntax. He's the guy under the sheet," said the guard with what appeared to be a leering grin.

Teresa moved up to the Commander and Bishop moved discreetly over to the stretcher to try and get a look.

"Hey, what do you want?" said one of the startled medics.

"Uh, nothing," said a dumbfounded Bishop.

Anderson shook his head and then indicated for the

other two to follow him. As they walked from the entrance Teresa spoke first.

"So he's dead, minutes before we arrive. Is it me or does that seen a little bit convenient?"

"Yeah, I think it's time we paid our friend Angelo a little visit!" said an angry looking Anderson.

CHAPTER TEN

Hundreds of years after the bayonet appeared irrelevant marines and soldiers throughout the Confederacy are still using it. Why still use them when modern body armour and weapons makes their use unnecessary? To quote a marine Captain, "What a thing guarding prisoners. The look on their faces when you have a 12 gauge shotgun with 17" of gleaming steel fixed to it----Priceless for compliance. There were Occasions when we fixed Bayonets during Cordon and Raids for the psychological fear they instilled…"

The Military Bayonet

Commander Anderson was first through the door and into the foyer. As he pushed through the crowd a concerned looking Teresa checked layout plans on her datapad. She'd already contacted Kowalski on the Tamarisk and a quick search had found the location of Maximilian Hex's apartment. Anderson had sent for Angelo and three of his best mercs to meet them there. As she finished checking the route she called out to the Commander.

"Are we sure we can trust them? What if they were behind this?"

"Who knows? Right now we need information and fast. The data I have on Angelo tells me he is unlikely to turn so easily. Either way, we'll know based on how he and his team responds at the room," he said as he stopped for a moment. He looked to the left and then back at the staircases. "Up the stairs, three floors and then past the security desk, right?"

"That's what Kowalski said," replied Teresa.

Bishop moved ahead and started climbing the wide, marble effect staircase. As they went up they were granted a perfect view of the elaborate foyer with its many people and large glass windows. As they reached higher it was possible to make out the glowing red feature of the burning planet of Prometheus below.

"You said you worked on that place?" asked a surprised looking Bishop.

"For a time, we moved around a lot. You can make a lot of money if you're in the right place and the right time down there," she explained.

"Yeah, I heard that. Unregulated private sector work with a high mortality rate. Sounds a bit like what we all do now!" he grinned as they reached the exit point on the third floor. "This is us."

Anderson moved towards the small security desk where a bored looking man sat watching a screen. He wore a grey suit and had no obvious weapons or armour. Behind him was a smart looking corridor with reflective metal surfaces and flushed door fittings spaced equally apart. It was undoubtedly one of the more expensive parts of the station.

"Can I help you?" asked the man.

Anderson was about to speak when a group of four men, all in smart suits approached. Teresa instantly recognised the face of Angelo leading them. Each of the men was tall and well built. To her they had the look of military or at least had been military in the past. Angelo moved closer and stopped next to the security man.

"Excellent, these are my guests from the trading floor, please buzz them in," he asked politely.

The guard tapped a few buttons and with a bored look waved them on. The three needed no reminder and moved quickly past the desk, following Angelo and his companions along the corridor.

"What was that all about?" asked Teresa.

"In this place it pays to have a cover. I've been working as a fixer for sometime now."

"A fixer?" asked Bishop.

"Yes. Someone who finds things or people then puts

them together with others for deal and contracts. You can find a bit of everything in this place, but you need to be able to open certain doors or to make contact with the right people. That is how I was able to get you access to the arms fair."

"Yeah, big help that was," snarled Bishop.

"I only heard about that a few moments after you left. It would appear contact was made from a source outside of this System that was acted on immediately. I have people investigating but I'm not hopeful. Someone didn't want you to find him and it looks like they made it with minutes to spare. Did you hear how he died?"

"Let me guess, an accident?" suggested Commander Anderson.

"Not quite, he was shot in the head with a military issue L48 carbine. Normally that wouldn't be so unusual, but there are now rumours spreading that Confed forces are moving onto the stations here. One thing they don't like out here is anybody telling them how to run things."

They continued in silence before coming to the end of the corridor that split off to the left and right. The route looked identical in either direction. Angelo indicated for them to turn left but before they could move one of his men flew back a metre and slumped to the ground dead. There was a hole the size of a tennis ball in his forehead.

"Back!" shouted the Commander as they all jumped for cover. With the corridor clear the only safety they had was to not move around the corner.

Teresa and Bishop both pulled out their concealed synthetic pistols. The weapons were small, snub-nosed affairs with small, low velocity disintegrating projectiles. They were useless for military operations but perfect for covert action, assassination or for getting through security clearance. They were also extremely expensive. A volley of almost silenced gunshots blasted down the corridor forcing the six of them to stay where they were.

"Somebody doesn't want us getting there!" shouted Bishop before leaning around the corner and firing three quick shots. The gun sounded like a hammer striking wood, the sound dull and unlike any other firearm. He ducked back.

"I can see three guys, they have a cabinet or something overturned and are hunkered down behind it. No way to hit them."

Angelo signalled to his two remaining men who pulled off their suit jackets to reveal body fitting ammunition belts and concealed fully automatic machine pistols. They pulled out the weapons and slammed in the long stick magazines. One leaned around the corner and fired a long burst as the second pulled a small hockey puck shaped grenade and hurled it along the corridor. The flash was followed by a concussive blast that shook the floor.

"Go!" shouted Angelo.

The two men with machine pistols pushed forward,

each of them firing bursts of two or three shots as they rushed the enemy position. Teresa followed, the rest were right behind her. In seconds they were over the cabinet and amongst the bullet-ridden corpses of their attackers. Three metres behind the men was the damaged doorway leading into Maximilian Hex's apartment.

"We won't have much time, private security around here is fast and violent, and I'd say four minutes, five tops."

As Commander Anderson rushed through the door he turned back to Angelo.

"Okay, you watch the corridor, we'll be three minutes and then we need to go, fast!"

As the three entered the room the excess immediately hit them. The space was voluminous, especially on a station where every cubic metre cost money. The walls were adorned with fine paintings and much of the furniture antique.

"We haven't got long, we need records, and any kind of data that can help us find the prisoners."

Teresa moved off towards the door to the bedroom and Bishop checked the furniture and floor for anything helpful. Some of the shelves had been forced, somebody, possibly the men from outside, had already been ransacking the place. As Teresa entered the bedroom she cried out and then went silent.

Bishop rushed closer and peered around the doorframe. A pistol shot blasted past and tore a painting from the wall.

"Come any nearer and the next one goes in her head!" shouted a man in the room.

Bishop turned to Anderson and indicated for him to take up position on the other side of the doorframe. Anderson lifted his hand, showing he was going to go high and Bishop low. With a final nod they counted with their hands and then rushed in. The man wore a suit and was holding Teresa up against the wall with a pistol to her temple. As they came in Teresa struck the man hard with her elbow, forcing the pistol away from her face for a brief moment. It wasn't much of a window but it was enough. Bishop fired a single shot into the man's chest that pushed him back, Commander Anderson placed a beautifully aimed shot into the man's forehead that sent a spray of blood and gore against the wall. Teresa jumped away from the carnage to stand next to Bishop.

"Thanks!" she laughed nervously.

Anderson was busy looking at a series of papers and a portable security terminal that the man must have been trying to leave with. His attention was caught by something on the display.

"What is it?" asked Bishop.

"It's still signed in, some kind of communication between this guy and a high security location."

"How can you tell?" asked Teresa.

"Well, for starters it says High Security Communication

along the top of the unit. There's a map showing several sites in this sector as well as a partially written message, look," he said as he lifted up the heavy unit and dumped it onto a worktop.

Bishop looked around the unit, checking it for signs of common connections or access points. As he examined the device he shook his head.

"Never seen anything like this."

"I have, these are used on ships and stations for encrypted communication between command units, whoever Hex was talking to was important. The map shows four locations. One is an underground site in Avagana, the second is an old research station below on Prometheus, the third is the Titan Naval Station and the fourth is an unidentified point 50AU away from Prime."

"Fifty? That is further out than all the planets? What is it?"

"Bishop, that I don't know," said Commander Anderson as he zoomed out and then zoomed down to the planet of Prime.

"Teresa, check this a moment, wouldn't you say this corresponds with…"

"The Bone Mill" she added before he could finish.

"Exactly. My hunch is these four sites are connected in someway with the insurgents. Titan Naval Station was obviously the location for a major insurgent action and for sometime was held by their forces. The Bone Mill is still a stronghold for their forces and if you remember was the launching point for a Biomech assault. This location on Prometheus is unknown but what are the odds it's equally involved?"

"Interesting. What about the location out in space? It could me a meeting point of some kind?"

"Why so far out though, Teresa? A reasonably fast ship would take about three weeks to make that trip. That would hardly useful for trading or transit. It must be something else."

"Have you seen this list of materials?" asked Bishop.

The three examined the document on the unit. It displayed a list of shipments of heavy materials, girders, security gear, metal plating and much more.

"This is big, really big. We're talking enough materials to build a medium sized space station and according to these logs it has all been going to one of the old compounds on Prometheus."

"It's unusual but why would that be anything to do with our mission, Sir?"

"Good point, Teresa. If you look at this list though you can see food, water and medical supplies going to the same place. More interestingly though is the quantities, this is more material than we needed for six months on the Crusader. We're talking about two thousand personnel there. This compound has been receiving more than that every week."

"Every week? That would mean they have thousand and thousands down there," added Bishop.

Anderson read a few more details before turning to Teresa.

"Teresa, get Angelo in here."

"You sure about that, Sir?"

"I think so, Bishop. They did their work here and lost a man in the process, we can't ask for more."

Teresa headed for the door as Anderson continued examining the computer system. Bishop moved to the stack of papers that had been in a briefcase and laid them out on the unit. As he shuffled through them Angelo arrived without his men.

"We can't stay any longer, have you got what you needed?"

"Just look at this, quickly!" said Anderson.

Angelo stepped forward and looked at the display. He traced the screen with his hand and seemed intrigued by the location on the planet surface.

"Interesting."

"What do you mean?" asked the Commander.

"We heard rumours sometime ago that something strange was going on at that place. We did land a team to investigate but all they found was a partially completed shipyard. It wasn't licensed, but then what is around here?"

"But look at the food and supplies being sent down there. No way can that just be a shipyard," said Anderson.

"What if they are sending human labour to the compound and using them in their production process?" suggested Teresa.

"What? Are you serious?" asked a surprised Bishop.

"Hold on, she has a point," said Angelo as he pulled out his own datapad and checked a few details. It took a few seconds before he brought up an image of a transport ship.

"We picked up a distress call from this area about an hour ago, the local rescue unit said they were responding so we ignored it. The interesting thing though is it is from the exact same location as where all these supplies were supposed to be heading. A report came in just before you contacted me to say it was a fire alert, nothing more serious. If you look at the logs on my datapad though, what do you see?"

Teresa examined the data but couldn't quite see the correlation.

"Look, on this transport route vessels move back and forth one a day. Since the alert came over a dozen ships have been making their way to the drop-off point to the planet. You see the ships need to drop smaller vessels to make the trip to the surface. If you ask me it looks like a force is assembling to be sent in."

Commander Anderson lowered the lid of the computer and turned to the group.

"A revolt with the workers down there?" asked Bishop.

"Or a riot?" added Teresa.

"Either way I think we have our location. Something big is going on down there and if we don't hurry it might be all over. Angelo, get your team assembled with full tactical gear and meet us at the Tamarisk in twenty minutes, I'll brief you when you get there."

"Don't you want to sent out scout drones first?"

"No, time isn't on our side. We'll sort out a detailed plan on the way. We're going to have to improvise on this one. Speed is of the essence and I have a few ideas about getting inside."

"Okay, it's your funeral. Twenty minutes." He turned and ran for the door.

"So, this is it then, Sir?"

"Yes, Teresa, grab what you can and follow me. It's time to go, come on," he said as he grabbed the briefcase and papers.

"About time, I just hope they're alive when we get there!" said an excited but fearful Teresa.

* * *

"Go, we'll cover you!" shouted Marcus.

Spartan, Misaki and Tigris rushed ahead and ducked down behind an overturned trolley. They had already covered most of the ground and so far run into just two guards who were quickly dealt with. At this point the main corridor opened up into the large ring section that occupied the centre of the base. From their position they could make out several dozen guards as well as columns of prisoners who were being escorted away, presumably to their cells. In the background the annoying hum of the compound alarm system wailed, indicating that a general alert was in progress. Spartan looked back at the rough note he had drawn on his arm.

"According to the security room this section opens out into the main ring. We'll have access to the harvesting areas and shipyards as well as the entrance to the computer centre. Can't we just sever the link somewhere?"

"No way. Did you see how far down the cabling goes? It's multithreaded as well, we take out one and they just shift the load onto a different circuit. The only option is to destroy or hijack the antenna masts or the computer centre. The masts are on the surface and exactly where reinforcements are likely to land," said Tigris.

"Yeah, but how the hell are we going to clear that area and get down to the computers? There must be over a hundred guards out there, look, see another group in armour?"

"Spartan, you need to do this one quietly," said Tigris.

Spartan gave him an odd look as Marcus joined in.

"The only way you'll get through there is if we get you a diversion. My recommendation is that you and Tigris hide here and we'll create a diversion and draw them back down the arm and towards the cells and security room."

"No way, you'll never hold them off."

"We don't have to, we just need you to get control of the computer system and comms. When you get there patch into the security feed and dump the video out on all frequencies. People need to know what these bastards are doing!"

Tigris looked at Marcus then back to Spartan.

"He's right Spartan, if we control the computer centre we will have full access to everything in this compound, including climate control, air filtration and pressure. We can hold the site to ransom or depressurise the whole place."

Spartan looked to the small group, trying to work out if this plan had any possibility of working. He never had the chance though as Gun made the choice for him and stepped out into the open roaring loudly. His voice must have attracted the attention of a score of guards as streaks of fire from projectile weapons blasted around them.

Spartan dove for cover, Misaki and Marcus moved to the side of the Biomech and joined in the shooting. Inside the great cavern the sound of the weapons was amplified substantially though nothing like the sound that came from Gun's Gatling gun. As he opened fire the entire group almost vanished in flame and smoke.

"Spartan, come on!" shouted Tigris who ducked down low and sneaked off around to the right, keeping his body low and in the shadows. Spartan followed and in just a few steps they were out of the line of fire and following round the perimeter. Every hundred metres or so, they were forced to stop as they reached a series of wide metal doors, each one easily able to accommodate a small transport vessel. Spartan turned to see Marcus disappear back down the corridor with Gun providing a devastating rear-guard. In front of them were at least twenty bodies and three times of that number were rushing after them.

"Look, that must be the entrance to the staircase right? We need to get there and then head down three levels. You ready?" asked Tigris before noticing that Spartan was still carrying the multi-barrelled gun given to him by the dying Biomech.

"What the hell did you bring that for?" he asked incredulously.

"This baby?" asked Spartan as he patted the metal of the barrels. "She might come in handy. Don't worry about me, I can handle myself."

Tigris shook his head in annoyance but Spartan simply ignored him and looked about the large open area, feeling exposed to attack at any moment. Their position was weak and vulnerable and he knew it.

"Wait a minute. We need to give ourselves a clear chance to make the distance. Look!" he said as he ducked back down pointing as discreetly as he could in the direction of the approaching men.

His timing couldn't have been better, another ten seconds and they would have run directly into the heavily armed group and their mission may have been over. As they kept low to the ground a group of six Zealots in their flowing robes and a dozen armoured guards ran past towards the doorway they had just passed. Spartan watched in fascination as one of them, the tallest of the group, pressed a series of buttons to open the seal. With a groan the massive door lifted up to reveal a great area, the equal of the hull of the ship they had arrived on. Hundred and hundreds of cylinders were laid out in the just the same fashion as he had already seen.

"Biomechs, they are making them here, poor bastards!" said an angry looking Spartan.

"Who cares about them, they're just meat, right now we have our own skins to save," said Tigris.

For a moment Spartan looked at the man in disgust, he had turned on his own and now had a callous disregard for the creatures being made here. His redeeming feature though was of course that he was helping them, maybe that was enough thought Spartan to himself.

"For now, we will be back to help them," said Spartan firmly. The more he thought about it though the more there was something in Tigris' tone that worried him. After his combat in space and then on Prime he had more reasons than most to hate the Biomechs. Yet he of all people could feel compassion for these manufactured slaves. One of them had already given its life for them and he had no doubt Gun would do the same. Tigris on the other hand seemed to be only interested in himself and would do whatever it took to stay alive. While their aims were remained in synchronisation, Spartan would stick with him, but with a watchful eye.

"Spartan, now!" shouted Tigris as he checked one last time and then dashed across the open ground. Spartan looked and followed, keeping low and moving as fast as his legs would carry him. They quickly made their way across the ground and reached the doors that led to the staircase system. The door was wide enough for three people to enter at once but like most of the compound it was locked.

"Can you open it?" asked Spartan as he looked behind them nervously. They were terribly exposed in this position and if they were located they would have no choice but to fight and die on the spot.

"No problem, the details from the security room should allow us access to most of the restricted areas," he said as he accessed the computer security system in the touch screen fitted to the wall. Spartan watched him work as he moved and rotated hexagonal icons around the screen until with a crunching sound the door opened to reveal a dark room with a narrow staircase going up and down. To the right were two locked elevators. Tigris moved directly past the door, calling out to Spartan as he made for the stairs heading down.

"Don't bother with the elevators, they are always locked down in an emergency."

* * *

"The signal is coming from the centre of this facility here," explained Commander Anderson as he showed his newly expanded crew the situation. As well as Bishop, Kowalski and Teresa there was also Angelo and his team of eight heavily armoured mercenaries.

"You're sure you want to hit this place? From your scans it looks like there could be thousands of people down there. What if they are all hostile?"

"Then this will be a really short trip, Angelo!" said an irritated Teresa.

"Hold on to your hats people, I'm picking up something!" shouted Kowalski as he moved through three pages of contact information.

"Yeah, look at this," he said as he brought up a three-dimensional model of the area around the planet. It showed six green contacts above the planet and directly above the compound.

"What are they?" asked Angelo.

"Cutters by the look of their size, about the same size as us. There are no Confed ships in this area, they must be private security," said Commander Anderson.

"Trust me, the private security around here you will not want to mess with!" replied a serious looking Angelo.

Teresa threw him a look of concern, for a moment worrying that the Commander might cancel the mission. If they were unable to complete this operation there was a very good possibility that they would lose the prisoners and that would be the end of Spartan and the rest of them.

"Nonetheless we're still going in!"

"What landing craft options do you have on this ship?"

"We have two shuttles, one a standard small crew civilian craft, the second a heavily modified black ops model. At a push you can fit six in each craft plus gear and weapons," said Bishop.

"That's not going to help us. How will we get the prisoners out with just two shuttles?"

"You won't, Angelo, for now your mission will be to secure access to the landing zones and attempt to find the prisoners. From the information we have there is something bad happening down there. Either there is an emergency or a riot and revolt of some kind. You land and then move in hard and fast. Get me intel and if you find the General get him to the surface. We can ferry up passengers with multiple passes, you might even be able to secure craft on the surface. As soon as you start your attack I will send a general Confed alert for assistance. Any police or off-duty forces are required to respond to the call and it might give us the extra numbers for the operation."

"We'll be in range in five minutes, Sir," said Kowalski as he monitored the displays.

"There is one other option," said Teresa.

"I thought there might be, what is it?"

"We could bring the Tamarisk down and land her, Sir. With her loading space and weapons we could take off any number of people and have the firepower to assist in an evacuation."

"No, not yet. We'll be a sitting duck to those ships in orbit. If we try and land we'll be shot down and lose everything. It is an option afterwards though," agreed Anderson as he brought up a view of the planet's surface.

"As you can see here there are a number of access doors, much like loading bay doors, at fixed intervals around a central landing pad. The central point is directly over the main power source and also beside the communications array. I suggest you form two teams. One will secure the communications array and the landing area. The second will penetrate the base and find our men."

"What about you, Sir?"

"I will stay with the ship, Teresa, and keep the cutters busy while you perform the drop."

"No way!" called Kowalski at the news. "That's a suicide mission, Sir, and one man can't do that, you'll be toast."

"Not necessarily, she's got more than they will be expecting and you will need the time on the surface."

"Commander, they have the numbers, I'll stay back and help with the operation. You need another set of hands for this one." Kowalski spoke in a tone that suggested he wouldn't take no for an answer.

The Commander considered his offer for a moment before accepting it.

"Okay, the two of us will provide a diversion by moving directly into the path of the cutters. I will trigger an electro-magnetic discharge that will scramble their sensors for up to a minute. That will be your window to start your attack run. All clear?"

Teresa, Bishop and Angelo all acknowledged him.

"Good, Bishop, you're the senior marine here, I want you leading the rescue team with Teresa as your second. You know our men and I know you'll do what needs to be done. Take half the mercs and the heavy weapons with you. You'll need them. Angelo, take the rest and keep that landing zone clear, it is critical for the retrieval of you all. If it falls apart you will rendezvous with Angelo and get the hell of that hot rock."

"We'll get them, Sir."

"I know you will, Teresa. Okay, get your gear and prepare your shuttles, how long do we have, Kowalski?"

"Three minutes, Sir, they've already picked us up and are scanning us."

Anderson turned to them. "Good luck, people, see you on the flip side!" he said with a grin.

Teresa and the others pulled themselves through the ship to meet the waiting mercenaries in the loading bay. It didn't take long for them to make it there. They were already wearing their armoured suits and just needed to grab their helmets before climbing inside the shuttles. Teresa tapped four of the mercs on the shoulders.

"You four are with us, we're on the rescue op the rest of you will be with Angelo and securing the LZ."

The mercs all looked to Angelo who gave them the nod. Teresa noted that they looked to him and not the marines. It wasn't really surprising, he had arranged their contracts, but it was of concern to her as to who could be fully trusted.

Reaching to the wall mounting she pulled off her helmet and pulled on the protective helmet. It took just seconds before they were ready for the vacuum of space and with simple hand signals they pulled themselves along to the two shuttles to get themselves ready for the operation.

Anderson looked over the computer screens and then to Kowalski.

"I'm going to put us right in the middle of the force. When I give you the signal you hit the trigger and send the pulse. If they look hostile we open up with everything we have, got it?"

"No problem, Sir, I've got the guns already loaded and the EM capacitors are on trickle charge, another minute they'll be ready."

"Good, this is going to be one hell of a surprise for them," said the mischievous Commander.

The communication screen started to flash to indicate an incoming message. Kowalski hit the button to show the feed but not to respond. The face of a Zealot, in the common robe they all seemed to wear, appeared.

"This is restricted territory. Please vacate this area immediately or you will be fired upon."

"Connect us," said Anderson as he quietly cleared his throat.

"This is Captain Mathius of the transport vessel Tamarisk. We have food and supplies for the compound below."

Kowalski grinned to himself as he watched the capacitor move further and further up.

"Tamarisk, you are not registered for any deliveries. Alter your course immediately or we will use deadly force."

Anderson grabbed the intercom. "Who the hell do you think you are? Under whose orders will you open fire?"

"The Church of Echidna is the only authority in this region. This is your final warning, Tamarisk." The signal was cut off abruptly.

"Commander, they are charging up their weapons, I am detecting railguns and missiles on two of the ships. Wait, what the…!" he cried hitting a button on the console quickly. An alert tone echoed through the ship and the emergency thrusters pushed the vessel slightly to one side as a projectile rushed past.

"They mean business, Sir, I think you can call that a shot across our bow!" he laughed.

"Yeah, you could say that. Standby on my mark, 5…4…3…2…1…now!"

Kowalski hit the release button and with a crackle a blast of energy rushed out from the ship in a large invisible bubble. A few sparks jumped from one of the broken computer units, next the navigation system and two displays went down.

Anderson reached for the intercom and spoke calmly, "Shuttles, you are a go, good hunting!"

* * *

Tigris and Spartan made it down to the three floors without issue and came to a rectangular room with doors on three sides. Each was mirrored like security glass but there were no obvious locks, hinges or doors. Tigris moved closer and struck his pistol against the toughened glass.

"Shit! It's a security screen, I've heard about them. They drop down to seal rooms against fire, water and gas." He stepped back and aimed into the middle of the door opposite him.

"What are you…" shouted Spartan before the loud crack of the pistol echoed in the room. He blasted it three times but the bullets did no more than take small chunks from the glass.

“Out of the way,” said Spartan as he swung his heavy Gatling gun into position. It was much too heavy to hold on the shoulder so he held it hung down next to his thigh. He pulled the trigger and with a deafening roar it spat out hundreds of large calibre heavy slugs that tore chunks from the glass. In seconds one pane was destroyed and he turned on the spot until the other two doors exploded into tiny shards. The gunfire halted but the barrels continued to turn as Spartan depressed the trigger.

“Nice!” shouted Tigris, as he stepped forward over the glass. Spartan dropped the gun, pulled out his side arm and followed him.

* * *

Teresa was first out of the shuttle, quickly followed by Bishop and the four mercenaries. With speed and precision they fanned out onto the landing platform. The second shuttle had just landed and she could just make out Angelo giving orders as the side door opened. She turned back and examined their surroundings. The landing platform was circular in shape and easily two hundred metres wide. To the one side was a large metal door recessed into the rock itself. A large communication array pushed up from the ground on the right with a series of antenna and dishes pointing up to the skies. The horizon was packed with rocky mountains, molten rock and burning fires.

"We're on Hell!" Bishop shouted through his headset.

Teresa turned back to the rest of the team, checking they were ready and fully armed. She carried an L48 carbine as well as several grenades mounted on her armour. In a holster on her hip was a P9 pistol, one of the items kept secure in the lockers of the ship.

"Let's go!" she cried and led the team towards the doorway. Bishop moved off to the left side of the door and pulled out a small case with a computer bypass unit installed. He attached a ribbon cable and fibre optic authenticator and started the procedure.

"How long?" asked one of the heavily armoured mercs.

"Hopefully not too long, our suits can't take this heat indefinitely," said Teresa as she checked the suit monitors.

As she stood waiting the door suddenly opened revealing a low ceiling and wide corridor that ran in a circle inside the structure. She turned back to see Angelo and his team fanned out and checking the perimeter. He spotted her and waved.

"Bishop, we've secured the platform but we can't stay out here, I suggest we move inside and guard the area from where you are. The heat will burn through these suits in ten to fifteen minutes."

"Do it!" he said and then turned to the corridor. He was first inside, quickly followed by Teresa and the mercs. After just a few hundred metres it was very clear something was going on. A number of bodies littered the ground and more could be found the further inside they went. One feature missing on their armour was any kind of external microphone system, though the suits were fitted with alarms in case of sound induced weapons. Checking the atmosphere was safe she flicked the release catch and pulled off her helmet. Fresh air washed to her face as well the dry heat from the planet. What really hit her though was the sound of gunfire and shouting. Bishop did the same though the mercs stayed fully sealed, she had no doubt their armour was more advanced and better equipped than hers. They all kept running, still finding nothing but the occasional body dressed in rags. She turned to Bishop.

"What the hell is going on here?"

"Get down!" he shouted as he jumped to the side and pushed her away. A blast from a powerful weapon knocked him back and to the ground. The mercs scattered and started to return slow but carefully aimed fire. Teresa lifted her carbine and scanned the area ahead. The winding path continued downwards into an area that looked like a giant circular racetrack. It must be the centre of the base as at least a dozen huge blast doors led off into corridors and rooms like the legs of a spider, her attention was caught by robed men carrying rifles. Two of them had spotted her team and were opening fire but the rest were shooting indiscriminately against people in rags and filth.

Teresa aimed carefully and squeezed off two rounds

into the closest man's face. The second was dropped by a fusillade from the mercs. With the immediate danger over the mercs pushed ahead to deal with the other guards as Teresa bent down to help Bishop up. Incredibly he was smiling.

"Don't worry, the armour did its job for a change!"

Teresa pulled hard and lifted him back to his feet. A fierce gun battle was going on between the guards and the mercenaries but the guards were completely outclassed and in less than a minute the route was clear.

"Where now, Teresa?"

"Good point, what do you think is happening here?"

"If you ask me I'd say this is a prison revolt, look," he said as he bent down to one of the bodies. The person was wearing ragged overalls and had rough, scarred hands. The woman had been shot three times in the chest and it looked like she had been trying to reach the surface.

"If it's a revolt then you can guarantee our people will be right in the middle of it. Look, over there!" She pointed towards more guards rushing through a wide doorway firing their weapons.

"Good idea, we can hit them from behind and roll them up till we find whatever the hell is going on here, come on!"

CHAPTER ELEVEN

Of all the characters in the sad tale of the Proxima Emergency it is that of the decorated Admiral Jarvis that is one of the most interesting. Prior to the troubles she had been due for early retirement for still unexplained reasons. Her quick thinking slowed the assault of the insurgents throughout Proxima and it is considered by many to this day that without her the System would have fallen within a month. It is only the long-term reputation of Spartan himself that finally overshadowed her ascendancy as his rise to pre-eminence became legendary.

The Fall of Admiral Jarvis

Alarms flashed throughout the bridge of the Tamarisk as she withstood barrage after barrage of weapon fire. In less than a minute of the battle starting she had sustained heavy damage and breaches in multiple quarters. One gun was knocked out and a fire was burning furiously in the spine of the vessel.

"Concentrate cannon fire on the closest cutter. Full burst then rotate ninety degrees and do the same to the next!" ordered the Commander as he altered their course to take them in closer to the group of vessels.

A violent crash smashed the Commander hard against the display and drew blood from his forehead. He wiped it aside and checked the screen.

"Bastards, they just hit our main engines with rockets. How many are left?" he asked, slightly confused from the strike.

"The first cutter is already a hulk, the second is burning from the inside out. Four remaining and they are closing in around us, Sir."

"I see them, hold on!"

He hit the evasive manoeuvres button that triggered the dorsal thrusters to pump a massive discharge of gas into space and forcing the vessel downwards. As they moved two cutters poured their volleys of railgun ammunition into each other. Kowalski redirected the automated turrets to continue their gunfire against the two disengaged ships, scoring good hits on both.

"Excellent work," smiled the Commander just as another hit struck the bow of their ship. Two of the displays blacked out followed by scores of red lights flashing across the consoles.

"Crap, we're got a problem!" shouted Kowalski.

Anderson tried to lean forward to examine the external camera feeds but strong g forces were forcing him into his seat.

Kowalski managed to get a screen up and started to trigger emergency control programs. "We've been hit in two of the stern propellant tanks, the escaping gas is putting us into a spin."

Another series of flashes sent sparks across the computers before the entire system went dead. A crunch like that of metal clamping against metal shook the ship and ever so slowly their spin slowed down.

Commander Anderson looked at the damage inside the vessel, just the red glow of the emergency lights remained. He could see the bloodied face of Kowalski and the significant damage inside.

"What's happening?"

"They're boarding us, Sir, they must be."

"No, they are not taking the Tamarisk! Break out the weapons, I'll start the auto destruct sequence."

Kowalski turned to him for a moment as the realisation that this could be the end of their mission occurred to him. The Commander gave him little chance to dwell on his thoughts.

"Kowalski, get going, now!" he growled.

* * *

Spartan and Tigris stood in the middle of the abandoned computer centre and looked about at the masses of equipment. The air-conditioned room was the coolest part of the compound and certainly the best maintained. In the centre of it stood three men, all dressed in suits and all visibly terrified at the sight of the two armed men.

"Who's in charge here?" demanded Spartan.

None of the men spoke but one looked over to a short, balding man. He was probably just looking for advice but it told Spartan all he needed. Marching over he placed his pistol to the man's forehead.

"Transfer full control of all the security points, cameras and doors to me!"

The man started to mutter, pleading innocence.

"Do it now, or this one eats a bullet," said Tigris as he dragged one of the men to the wall and push him face first against it.

"Well?" asked Spartan.

The man hesitated for just a few seconds. "Okay, okay, come with me."

The man, obviously terrified, led Spartan to one of the computers and sat down. With a flurry of hand movements he started to move control of all the systems to the computer centre. On the screens nearby Spartan could make out the running battles that were now raging throughout the compound. The sector he had been secured inside was definitely the focal point of the conflict and hundreds appeared to be engaged in a brutal and bloody battle.

"I want full control of the scrubbers, climate control and air vents."

"What?" the man asked.

A bang shook the room and the man Tigris had been threatening slumped to the floor, a dark red pattern of blood and gore running down the wall. Spartan shook his head, the more time he spent with Tigris the more he doubted the man's sanity.

"Okay, I'm doing it! It will take a few minutes for access to the circulation and airlock system to transfer!"

"Where are the controls for the shipyards, the factories, the machines?" demanded Spartan before the man could turn away.

"Uh, we just manage the computers. The overall control comes from the Core."

"What do you mean, the Core?" shouted Tigris from where he stood.

"The Governor, us, the guards, we're all just custodians for the system. The factories are maintained by us but the orders come directly from the Core through the communication system."

"Where is it?"

The man shrugged, "Really, I have no idea, we aren't

given that kind of information."

Spartan tilted his gun slightly and gave the man a look that told him either he told the truth or he would be joining his comrade.

"I promise you, I do not know!" he cried.

Spartan relented and lowered the pistol to leave the man to carry on with his work. He worked fast and it didn't take long before Spartan had full control of all the systems for the compound. He checked the screen to get an idea how the revolt was going, it wasn't easy but from what he could see it looked like a stalemate. For now that was okay but he knew that the ships in orbit would soon start dropping in reinforcements, then it would all be over.

"You, over here!" Spartan shouted as he beckoned for the other man to come forward. "You will patch all of the video feeds, including the harvesting rooms and these prison areas. Link them together into an unencrypted packet and start transmitting the data on all channels."

The man looked to his supervisor who nodded furiously.

"Good, now, I have another job for you. Find me that bastard the Governor, we have things to discuss," he said angrily.

"I thought we were going to hold them to ransom?" asked Tigris.

"We will but it's going to take a few minutes to get full control. Plus, we need to find that bastard first before we can negotiate."

"It's working," said the one of the men as he pointed to the screens.

"What exactly?" asked Spartan.

"The transmission, I'm sending the signal you wanted, it is being sent out to the Trading Station, outposts and any ships within range."

"Good, attach a message explaining what this place does. Don't try and be smart-ass, we have military units on the way and those who help us now might avoid consequences later on. Understood?" he said winking at Tigris.

"Okay, I know about the Biomechs and the ships, we were forced to work here like all the other prisoners," he said, though Spartan looked less than convinced.

"What are you waiting for?" was his only reply.

"Hey, Spartan, have you seen what's going on at Screen 13?" asked Tigris.

Spartan shook his head and stepped back to take a look at the display. It was the large corridor that ran from the security room and towards the centre of the base. About a hundred prisoners along with the bulk of what must be Gun were hunkered down behind an improvised barricade of containers, broken machinery and bodies. Attacking them were double their number of guards and Zealots along with a sprinkling of Biomechs. The defenders appeared to have the better position though and were managing to hold them back. Spartan looked closely, he was sure he could see the figure of General Rivers next to the creature waving something and shouting.

"The crazy old man, he's always in the middle of trouble," said Spartan to himself. "Look, is that who I think it is?"

Tigris looked at the enemy reinforcements that surged through the corridor to assault the barricade. In the middle was the unmistakable shape of the Governor.

"There he is!" said Tigris with venom. "I want him!"

"Easy now, there's time, first we've got to get control of the facility, then we can finish him off."

"Fine, you stay, I'm out of here!" shouted Tigris and then he was gone.

Spartan looked about the room and then to the two men at the computers.

"How long till I get control?"

The one man turned back to Spartan, "It's yours, I can put the control to a portable device if you want?" The man was obviously trying to appease him.

"You can transfer control to a datapad?"

"Sure, give me a few seconds."

It took just a few taps before he turned back and handed him a ruggedised datapad that was locked into the system. Spartan looked at the screen and noted the complete structure of the base, it looked even bigger than he expected.

"Just tap the area or system and you can issue commands

directly to the computer centre."

"Good, come on, upstairs!" he said as moved back to the broken glass and in the direction Tigris had taken.

As the three left the room the largest screen showed the raging battle around the barricade. A small monitor showed the video feed back towards the centre of the compound where six armoured warriors were engaged with the Zealots in a bitter firefight. Spartan spotted the action from the corner of his eye and quickly pulled himself back. As he did so the two men ran for it, he lifted his pistol and pointed it at the back of the closest. He started to pull the trigger but stopped, he wouldn't kill them, not yet anyway. Looking back at the screen he tried to work out who the six were. Tapping the display the camera zoomed in to show the six in body armour and military grade firearms. At the front were a man and woman, both without helmets and firing carbines. He almost fell over when he spotted the woman's face.

"Teresa!" he shouted.

Without pausing he turned and ran for the stairs.

* * *

Teresa ducked as a Zealot swung what could only be described as a sharpened halberd at her head. Her speed saved her but not the mercenary who took the full impact in his shoulder. Even his toughened synthetic body armour could not stop the razor sharp crystal edged blade from cutting deeply into his flesh. As he dropped in agony he lifted his carbine and tore the man in half with a deadly burst of gunfire.

"Bishop, what's the plan!" she shouted, firing a short burst at another Zealot as he emerged from cover.

They had reached the mouth of the corridor and run directly into a group of reinforcements that appeared to be involved in a major battle further inside the compound. As the last Zealot was cut down her team moved to the walls and looked inside the corridor at the unfolding battle. Two of the mercs dragged the wounded man to cover before joining them.

"I don't know, we can join this fight but it could be nothing to do with our mission, what if this is just some kind of labour dispute?" he asked before lifting his carbine and pointing it behind Teresa.

"Hey, who are you?" he shouted as a man, half dressed in the garb of one of the guards approached with raised hands.

"The name's Tigris, I was going to ask you the same. I'm helping with the escape, you here to help?"

"We're looking for a Confed General and a group of prisoners."

"A General, well, I've been working with a guy called Spartan, I know he's with a group of Confed guys, most of them are back there in the fight."

Bishop turned to Teresa who pulled back the bolt on her carbine and rushed after the enemy reinforcements.

"Come on!" shouted Bishop before Tigris was able to explain further.

The surviving mercenaries followed, each of them continuing their carefully aimed shooting and started to pick off the guards and Zealots from behind. In less than a minute the enemy's numbers had been halved before they even realised there was somebody behind them. In the middle a small group of Biomechs looked like they had gone on the rampage, there were three and all of them had turned on the Zealots, one with a Gatling gun tore a dozen men to shreds. In the middle a man in a suit stood calmly and shouted for them to stop. A few guns stopped but one of the Biomechs continued to fight before being dragged to the ground by half a dozen Zealots. They were about to finish the creature off when the man called out.

"Stop this madness, immediately!"

The gunshots had all but stopped and the remaining thirty of the enemy moved back slightly, taking up positions in cover as the leader followed them. The Biomechs stayed where they stood, neither following the enemy nor joining the defenders on the barricades.

"I am the Governor and you will lay down your weapons immediately. This act of sedition is punishable by exposure to the surface!" he roared.

One of the defenders fired a shot that just missed the

man and was immediately hit in the forehead by a return shot from one of the guards.

"At this very moment a dozen warships are bringing hundreds of reinforcements to quell this little revolt of yours. Surrender now and you can return to your cells, keep fighting and you will all be executed, including those still in their cells."

From her position Teresa could make out people moving back and forth though it wasn't clear what they planned to do. As she contemplated what to do the newly arrived guard stepped past her and towards the Governor.

"Governor, I've made contact with the enemy, I know who they are and their plans."

The Governor turned and smiled at him.

"Excellent, so our little group have given up their contacts in the Confederacy. Good work, this news will greatly assist in our struggle," he said as he indicated for Tigris to move to the side and out of the way of likely gunfire.

"Governor, this is General Rivers, Commander of Confed ground forces. Surrender now and I guarantee you a fair trial!" came a booming voice behind the barricades.

Teresa's heart lifted as she recognised the voice.

"Governor, you bastard, turn around!" roared a voice she knew even better.

Turning she spotted the bloodied figure of Spartan. His clothes were ruined and blood dripped down his face.

In his hand he carried a rifle, presumably taken from one of the many fallen guards. The man turned around to face Spartan, a look of amusement on his face.

"Well, well, I see you have…" he started before being cut short by a single shot to the head. Blood burst from his skull as he dropped lifelessly to the ground. With their leader gone the remaining guards surrendered, leaving just around ten Zealots who backed away, looking for a way out.

Spartan looked over towards Teresa who stood holding a smoking carbine, still pointing at the body of the Governor. Bishop stood next to her. From behind the barricade the remaining people jumped down and rushed towards Spartan and the other survivors. General Rivers, sporting half a dozen minor wounds was helped down and limped towards Teresa. Spartan also spotted Marcus and Misaki. A loud roar came from the defenders followed by Gun who jumped over the metal obstacle and landed just a few metres from Teresa. She lifted her gun ready to fire again, only to be stopped by the strong arms of Spartan who grabbed her tightly.

"I knew you'd be in the middle of this!" she laughed.

As the two embraced, General Rivers approached with Misaki and Marcus.

"Ahem!" coughed the General, trying to get Spartan's attention.

It seemed nothing would split them apart until finally

Teresa pulled back, spotting the figure of the General. She saluted smartly, Spartan pushed out his hand and shook it

"Excellent work, both of you. Can I assume, Private, that your appearance here is the precursor to Confed troops arriving?"

Teresa looked back to Spartan, her eyes alive with pleasure and then back to the General.

"We came on the Tamarisk, Sir, just two shuttles. How many people are here?"

"Thousands, Private, tens of thousands. We can't leave, not yet," he said firmly before turning to Spartan.

"Did you get the signal out?"

"Yes, Sir, it's already being transmitted on all frequencies."

Bishop stepped forward, saluting the General.

"Sir, you might want to hear this," he said as he held out his intercom unit.

"Commander Anderson here. Your signal got out. There are over twenty civilian ships in orbit demanding the Echidna vessels leave immediately. Apparently your footage is causing uproar on the Trading Post. There's talk of an outright ban on the Church and its associates throughout the Prometheus System."

There was a short burst of static before he continued, "We will be landing shortly. What is your status?"

"We have the prisoners, a lot of them," said Spartan almost excitedly.

"Good, we won't be taking off anytime soon though, the ship's badly damaged."

"You and Kowalski?"

"We're okay, Sergeant, I have to go, this is going to be an interesting landing, Tamarisk out."

Bishop took back the intercom unit and fitted back his armour.

General Rivers looked over to Bishop.

"Thank you, son, your team have done the Confederacy proud. I need you to help arrange triage for the wounded and we have to get in touch with friendly vessels in the area. There are a lot of hurt people down here. Spartan, can you patch me through to our Communication Post on the Trading Station? I need to get word to the Admiral about this place."

"Sir!"

"Look out!" shouted Teresa as she spotted Tigris moving out from the shadows with a pistol pointed at General Rivers' head. She grabbed at her pistol but it was too late. A bright light engulfed the traitor before scattering his body into a dozen pieces across the floor. She looked across to the smiling Biomech whose gun was still rotating giving off smoke.

"That's Gun by the way, our new best friend!" said Spartan who then grabbed Teresa again and pulled her close.

General Rivers moved away to speak with Bishop and

the scene quickly turned from one of carnage to one of recovery and repair. As the General walked away he left Misaki stood, staring at the two with a look of anger on her face. With a growl to herself she stormed off to join the others.

"Hey, you crazy woman!" Marcus finished tying the bonds on two of the Zealots and ran over to Teresa and Spartan.

Teresa hugged him so hard he groaned. As he pulled away she looked at them both.

"You two don't get away that easily," she said with a laugh and then held them both tightly.

* * *

Admiral Jarvis paced inside the CiC of the newly repaired and now fully operational CCS Crusader. It had taken weeks to finish the repair work but with her now ready for battle the Admiral finally had a fleet worthy of the Confederacy. Over a dozen capital ships sailed alongside her as they made their way to their rendezvous with the CCS Wasp and her extra forces.

"General, the information you obtained from Prometheus is fascinating. As per your recommendations the Biomech programming has been reversed though what we will have to do when they are hatched, for want of a better word, is something we will have to consider.

The total count of prisoners released will be in the thousands. Thankfully the video footage has created uproar throughout System," she said with glee.

"That is good news, Admiral, will this turn the tide?"

She stood, silent for a moment as she looked at the strategic map of the Proxima System. Nothing had changed in terms of control of territory but the propaganda victory couldn't be overstated.

"News from my contacts at Fort Hood on Kerberos tells me there have been several popular uprisings against the new government and their rulers. It isn't the end, not by a long shot, but I truly believe this is the best opportunity we have had for months. How is the team? I understand they are back on the Santa Cruz recovering?"

"Yes, the entire group were commendable and I have requested promotion for them all. Especially Sergeant Spartan and Private Morato. They proved strong and dependable in a critical situation."

"Indeed, I understand my old friend Commander Anderson is still on the planet working through the shipyard intelligence?"

"Yes, when he saw some of the half completed vessels I couldn't get him to leave," he said with a grin.

The intercom on the wall started to emit a tone. The Admiral walked over and picked it up, she listed for a moment then replaced it.

"General, the probe is due to enter the anomaly in the

next minute."

The entire CiC was empty other than the two commanders and one trusted science officer who managed the probes support system. On the screen between them the image flipped from the strategic map to a full size time-delayed video feed from their probe.

"This is the anomaly Commander Anderson obtained intelligence on?" he asked. The science officer nodded in agreement.

"Does it correlate with the intelligence we received from our source on Kerberos?"

"Yes, Sir, it is positioned roughly 50AU from Prime. We tracked the surviving cutters from the battle over Prometheus making their way to the point before losing contact with them."

"Special Agent Johnson managed to get additional location data to us from Fort Hood before the planetary transmission was jammed. Whatever it is, the insurgents don't want us finding out about it," explained the Admiral.

"What is it? Some kind of cloaked or masked base?"

Admiral Jarvis shrugged.

"Admiral, the probe has just past through the path of a massive digital transmission, it is coming from the anomaly. We only have a small fragment of the data, it appears to be encrypted control code for automated systems, I have sent it to the decryption analysis engine for study," the Science Officer said, pressing several buttons on his console. Just seconds later he turned back to the Admiral. "The probe is entering the anomaly in ten seconds."

The three stopped what they were doing and watched the video feed. They had no idea what to expect other than it was the unknown.

"Strange," said the Science Officer, "the probe is still accelerating, it should be…" he said as the image flashed and showed several bright colours and then went black.

"Signal lost, Admiral."

General Rivers appeared unmoved but Admiral Jarvis shook her head in annoyance and turned away.

"I knew we should have sent something slower. Six days for the probe wasn't enough in my opinion, it must have hit something on its arrival."

"Uh, Admiral, you need to see this."

Admiral Jarvis turned back, intrigued by the tone of the man's voice.

"Yes?"

"Look, if I move one frame at a time there are three frames after the flash on arrival."

"Okay, what is it?"

The officer brought up the first image. It was nothing other than a multicolour blue blur. The second image was dark blue with a few patches on it and the third was just noise.

"Can you enhance the second one?"

"I'll see what I can do, Admiral." He started fiddling

with his computer.

Admiral Jarvis moved to the next computer and started trawling through astronomical objects before settling on one. She hit a key and blew it up full size on the main view screen.

"Well, how long?"

"It will take a few hours to fully compile, this is what I have so far though." He loaded the partially enhanced image to the screen next to the one the Admiral had used.

"Are you seeing what I am, Admiral?" asked a bewildered General Rivers.

"Quite, if I'm not mistaken, that is Terra Nova."

"The capital of Alpha Centauri?" asked the confused Science Officer.

Admiral Jarvis stepped back and examined the images side by side.

"It looks to me like we have just discovered a viable route that leads directly to Terra Nova. If it works we can travel between both points in weeks instead of nearly a year." She turned and looked at the General.

"This is sensational. We must assemble a fleet and move to control this position immediately. If this anomaly truly works, it will be the single most important piece of real estate in the entire sector. We and nobody else must control it. This could be our lifeline to the old worlds and the key to our final victory!"

She stopped for a moment as she considered their

position before looking at the images again.

"You being captured may have been the best thing that ever happened to us!" she said happily.

CPSIA information can be obtained at www.ICGtesting.com
Printed in the USA
LVOW061704011112

305252LV00004B/39/P

9 781906 512774